CW00519548

Grahame C. W. Howard was born in London in 1953. His family moved to Norwich when he was four but he returned to London to study Medicine at St. Thomas' Hospital in 1970. Following a series of junior doctor posts in London and Cambridge, he was appointed consultant clinical oncologist in 1986. His first book, *The Tales of Dod* was published in 2010.

To the boys: Richard, Michael and Charles.

GRAHAME C. W. HOWARD

THE NORRIS SANCTION

AUSTIN MACAULEY PUBLISHERS™

LONDON • CAMBRIDGE • NEW YORK • SHARJAH

A CIP catalogue record for this title is available from the British Library.

ISBN 9781528936866 (Paperback)
ISBN 9781528936873 (Hardback)
ISBN 9781528968874 (ePub e-book)

www.austinmacauley.com

First Published (2021)
Austin Macauley Publishers Ltd
25 Canada Square
Canary Wharf
London
E14 5LQ

My grateful thanks go to June for her support and I am greatly indebted to Millie Gray for her help and encouragement over the years.

Chapter 1

It's quite extraordinary how the most mundane and seemingly insignificant of events can result in unexpectedly devastating consequences. How a chain of actions, ultimately resulting in disaster, can be triggered by a small, apparently insubstantial act. A ship is lost for a ha'porth o' tar; a butterfly flaps its wings in South America resulting in an earthquake in Asia; or was it a tsunami in the Philippines? I don't recollect but it matters not: it's the principle that I'm trying to convey. In a similar vein, it is also true that the initial event may be so trivial that it passes unnoticed, only to be recalled when its profound and unexpected consequences are realised, often separated widely in time and space.

In the case of Andy Norris, on that fine early spring evening in 1974, it was the consistency of the batter which coated his piece of plaice that would change his life forever. If the batter had been crisper; if Abdul, the proprietor of the North Sea Fish Shop on Clapham Common South Side, had immersed the fish in his deep-fat fryer for just one minute longer, then the series of events that I am about to relate would never have been initiated and Andy would have been shot before he had taken his first mouthful. As it happens, this was not the case and the batter was ever so slightly soggier than usual, to a degree where it did not have the structural integrity to maintain the shape of the portion of fish against the force of gravity.

Thus it was that when Andy settled himself on the park bench on the periphery of Clapham Common in pleasant anticipation of his supper and lifted the piece of battered fish towards his mouth, it began to sag. In a split second, Andy, who was an experienced consumer of fish and chips, realised that without immediate restorative action, his piece of fish would break in half and the section destined for consumption would fall back into his lap where the rest of his supper now lay exposed in the previous day's edition of the *London Evening News*. Andy therefore bent his head quickly in order to grab the drooping fish in his jaws and this sudden movement resulted in the bullet, which had been destined for his left temple, passing unnoticed behind him only to lodge itself, with dire consequences, into the head of a vagrant Irishman who was sitting at the opposite end of the park bench.

Having safely retrieved the piece of fish, Andy turned to offer his companion a chip. To say that he was surprised to find the vagrant dead would be an understatement. The Irishman, who wintered in the south of London and with whom Andy often shared a fish supper and a can of beer, was now lolling against the side of the bench, a small hole in the side of his head and a surprised look on his face.

In later life, when Andy recalled the events of that spring, he never ceased to be amazed how, over the period of a few short weeks, his life had been turned upside down through pure chance and a case of mistaken identity.

***

Just a week before the incident involving the soggy fish batter, Andy Norris had been unconcernedly pursuing his ambition-free existence.

'Zeph, put a record on, mate. It's too quiet in here.' Andy pushed some ten-pence coins across the table towards the man sitting opposite him. He was right; the Herald Lounge Bar situated in Lombard Street in the heart of the City of London was empty apart from the two of them and as well as being quiet, it felt unwelcoming and smelled faintly of disinfectant. Zephaniah was the night porter at Global Insurance, the same company that employed Andy to maintain their computer systems. Directly after finishing his day's work at around five o'clock, Andy would generally walk the hundred or so yards to the Herald where more often than not, he would find Zephaniah, a burly middle-aged Afro-Caribbean, studying the next day's racing form on his way to work.

The Herald Lounge Bar was a soulless, tacky establishment. Full of mirrors, plastic and chintz, it exemplified all that was bad about public houses newly built in the seventies. The very fact that it called itself a lounge bar rather than a pub said it all. With its pretentious décor, gassy beer and phoney cocktails, this was not a watering hole for bankers and traders but a meeting place for petty criminals and wide boys. Dressed in sharp suits and smelling of Brut aftershave, this was where would-be gangsters congregated with their trouser-suited, permed girlfriends to hear the latest gossip, listen to the jukebox and do a bit of business. If you wanted to buy a gun or put the frighteners on someone, this was the place to make such arrangements.

Andy, who was an enthusiastic and discerning beer drinker, hated the bar but was too lazy to go anywhere else. Situated on the corner of Lombard Street and Birchin Lane, it was ideally placed to break his short journey from Global Insurance to Bank Station where, five or six pints and half a packet of Embassy Specials later, he would board a tube for Clapham Common. It was there that he lived in rented accommodation with a secretary who worked for a local law firm and a medical student. Thus, it was to the Herald Bar that he would habitually gravitate after a day toiling with malfunctioning computer programmes to read the newspaper, drink a few pints and chat intermittently with Zephaniah.

'*You* put it on, man.' Zeph did not look up from his copy of the *Racing Times*.

Andy sighed, put his newspaper down on the stained table next to his half-full pint mug and wandered over to the jukebox. He peered at the rows of small typed cards on either side of the record arm. 'What d'you fancy, Zeph? *The New Seekers* or *Mrs Mills plays Christmas Tunes*?'

'Anything as long as it ain't Mrs Mills. She shouldn't be allowed, man. Anyway, Christmas is long gone.'

'But the spirit of Christmas lives on, Zeph, through Mrs Mills and Slade, who are, by the way, still at number one.'

Andy looked towards his friend who was studiously ignoring him.

Andy turned his attention back to the jukebox and selected three tunes before strolling back to the table where he picked up his mug and swallowed the remaining contents. 'Another one, Zeph?' he asked as he headed towards the bar.

'Yeah, man. Make it a rum and coke.'

Back at their table, Andy took a swig from his beer, lit a cigarette and settled back in the imitation leather seating which ran around the periphery of the room. He opened his copy of the *London Evening News* where a headline caught his attention. 'Crumbs, Zeph! That man, Vinnie Archer, has shopped his mate, Kenny Craft.'

Zephaniah looked up from his *Racing Times*. 'I know, man, I saw it on the news last night. He used to drink in here.' He turned his concentration back to his paper, adding knowingly, 'He's dead', before continuing to circle the names of horses with a red crayon in preparation for the next day's bets.

'Who's dead?' Andy looked up from his paper, puzzled.

'Vinnie – the *Bowman* – Archer; just as soon as Kenny Craft gets out.'

'Yeah. But not for a long time. Kenny's gone down for ten years.'

Zephaniah didn't raise his eyes from the *Racing Times*. 'Maybe, man, but I wouldn't want to be Mr Archer when Kenny's released.'

Two more pints and an hour later, Zephaniah announced that he was leaving for his night shift. Andy bade him farewell and glanced at his watch where Mickey Mouse's arms indicated that it was nine o'clock: *Time for one more pint, then home,* he thought. Half an hour later, he walked slightly unsteadily out of the bar and headed towards Bank Station.

Andy was an untidy human being. It wasn't just his clothes, which undoubtedly were dishevelled, but his whole life was rather disorderly. The suit, which he habitually wore for work, was creased and stained. His shirt wasn't ironed and was one of those styled as 'slim-line', a design suited to thin Italian teenagers and not plump, out-of-condition Londoners. It failed miserably to encompass his ample girth, resulting in an expanse of flesh poking through the lower buttons where it flopped lazily over his belt. His tie, stained by numerous fish suppers, ketchup and beer, was knotted an inch below his unbuttoned collar. On his plump but not unpleasant face, he habitually wore a vacuous expression as though he wasn't wholly aware of what was going on around him – not quite in touch with the rest of humankind. His thick, curly dark hair flopped untidily over his eyes, his ears and the collar of his jacket.

At twenty-six years old, he had happily settled into a comfortable, if boring, lifestyle and his sole aim in life was to maintain the *status quo*. His existence comprised of commuting to the city every morning, maintaining the computer systems of Global Insurance until five o'clock before proceeding to the Herald Lounge Bar, where he would read the newspaper, chat to Zephaniah while drinking and smoking until it was time to catch a tube back to Clapham Common from where he would walk home, normally via the North Sea Fish Bar.

That evening, a week before his attempted assassination, he negotiated the barriers, escalators and tunnels of Bank Tube Station without conscious thought. He had done it so often and in such advanced states of inebriation that he could probably have done it blindfolded. He waited just two minutes for a grimy southbound Northern Line train, which he boarded before slumping on to a seat where he sat staring vacantly at the opposite window until he reached Clapham Common station where he alighted. On more than one occasion, he had fallen asleep on the tube and had awakened to find himself at Morden: the end of the line. There, most of the staff knew him and would direct him to the opposite platform and settle him back on a northbound train if they were still running.

As he left the station and stepped on to the brightly illuminated pavement, he breathed in the fresh spring air, crossed the road and joined the queue inside the North Sea Fish Bar. After shuffling forward slowly for several minutes, he reached the stainless-steel counter above which hot glass cabinets housed all manner of delicacies. There, battered cod, skate and plaice lay enticingly alongside saveloy, cod's roe and meat pies.

'Evening, Abdul. Plaice and chips please.'

Abdul looked at him and smiled. 'Two minutes, Andy,' he said.

Andy took a seat on one of the tall stools at the window of the fish shop and gazed out across the busy road to the darkness that was Clapham Common. Five minutes later, with an open newspaper full of fish and chips in one hand, a lit cigarette and a piece of fish in the other, he wandered fifty yards along the broad pavement before turning left onto a quiet crescent. Three houses along, he proceeded up a short path to the front door of a detached house where a sign above the door proclaimed it to be Parkview Cottage. Here, Andy struggled with his fish supper and cigarette while searching his pockets for his door key, spilling a significant proportion of his meal on the doorstep in the process.

Safely inside, he kicked the front door shut behind him, negotiated a short hallway and entered the sitting room. There, a pretty woman in her early twenties wearing a dressing gown and a towel wrapped around her head turban-style, was sitting watching television, her feet curled under her and a mug of coffee in her hand.

'Hi, Lucy,' Andy said as he flung himself on to the vacant settee and continued to eat what was left of his fish and chips.

The girl did not take her eyes off the television. 'Hi, Andy. Are you pissed again?'

'No. Are you?'

The girl did not answer.

'Anyway, there's nothing wrong with winding down with a pint or two after a hard day at the office.'

The girl looked at him and grimaced. 'Nah, course not. Although with you, it's a pint or ten most nights.'

Andy looked up from his supper. 'That, Lucy, is an outrageous calumny and entirely unfounded. When have I ever returned home pissed?' retorted Andy who then belched loudly.

'Every day this week so far and most of last, now I come to think about it.'

'Yes; but apart from those rare occasions, I remain the epitome of an upstanding, morally...' Andy paused in an attempt to find an appropriate word and then gave up, '...something. Anyway, how was *your* day?'

'The usual.' Lucy was quiet for a moment before adding, 'There's a new partner in the firm. Really 'andsome 'e is.'

Andy frowned. 'What, more handsome than me?'

'Andy, *everyone* is more 'andsome than you.' Lucy smiled at her housemate. 'I'm sure you've got attributes, Andy. It's just that no one's found them yet, that's all.' Lucy fell silent as she concentrated on the television. 'Ooh, look! Kenny the Giant Craft 'as been sent down for ten years.'

After picking the last crumbs of batter from the newspaper, Andy scrunched it up noisily and threw it in the general direction of a bin in the opposite corner of the room where it fell to the floor next to a crumpled copy of the previous week's *Sunday Times* and some empty beer cans. 'Why do they all have to have these idiotic epithets: Vinnie – the *Bowman* – Archer; Kenny – the *Giant* – Craft?'

'It's part of the East End gang culture, Andy. You wouldn't know, coming from Enfield an' all.'

'We had our criminals in Enfield, I'll have you know. Someone robbed a newsagent once.' Andy was thoughtful for a moment. 'Come to think of it, for a while I was known as Andy – the *Loser* – Norris.' Andy was pensive for a moment and then looked at Lucy. 'Did you know that the first ATM was installed in Enfield? And another thing, Sir Joseph Bazalgette was born there. What d'you think of that?'

Lucy continued to concentrate on the television, 'Who on earth was 'e?'

'Built London's sewage system, that's all.'

But Andy knew that Lucy was right. Being born and brought up within the periphery of Greater London did not make you a Londoner. The problem was that it did not make you a non-Londoner either. You were just part of the amorphous mass of people that populated the southeast of England. You had no history or culture of your own. Apart from the builder of sewers, Andy could not recall any other famous sons of Enfield; whereas Lucy, born in Wapping, was a proper East-ender and had the accent to prove it. As a child and young woman, she had mixed with gangsters and criminals. Now, working as a secretary for a Clapham firm of solicitors, she was living in the relatively bourgeois grandeur of South London. Clapham could be rough but it was nothing compared to Wapping, and Parkview Cottage was luxury compared to her parents' tenement.

Chapter 2

Police Constable Crocker was an uninspiring person caught in the throes of an unspectacular career. That is, until he accidentally played a pivotal role in the capture and subsequent conviction of the well-known gangster, Kenny Craft. After leaving school at sixteen with four O levels (the most academic of which was geography with the others being religious instruction, woodwork and art), he had eventually been accepted by the police force. That had been ten years ago and his progress through the ranks of the Metropolitan Police Force had been slow. In fact, it was not just slow, it was non-existent. Not known for his crime-solving abilities, he had spent the last ten years filling in lost property forms, searching for missing dogs and very occasionally investigating a break-in. He knew that policing could be more exciting, having seen it on television. Crocker saw himself in the role of one of the cops in *The Sweeney*, driving fast cars, performing screaming handbrake turns, then screeching to a halt before leaping out, crouching behind the bonnet and shooting some passers-by.

Slightly built and prematurely bald, Crocker looked more like a bank clerk or curate than an undercover policeman but that did not deter him from slipping on a pair of faded blue jeans, lacing up his pumps and donning his pride and joy – a bomber jacket – at the weekends. He would then slip on a pair of sunglasses and emulate his heroes by driving his pale blue Ford Anglia around the South Circular, sometimes reaching speeds of nearly sixty miles an hour. Twice, he had requested a secondment to the Flying Squad, only to be turned down and he knew that opportunities for his advancement were receding as time progressed. However, it is a strange fact of life that the less achievable a goal is, the more a person will yearn for it. Thus, PC Crocker still nurtured his ambition to be an undercover, gun-toting, crime-busting cop.

The problem was that his colleagues, and more importantly his superiors, recognised a very different Crocker. They saw him as a desk-bound pen-pusher who could not catch a criminal even if one came up to him with 'I'm a criminal – please arrest me', tattooed on his forehead. However, everyone at some stage in his life gets a lucky break and PC Crocker's finally came in the late summer of 1973. He had been asked to investigate a bicycle theft that had occurred outside a pub in the city of London. The owner of the bike resided in Clapham so the crime was considered to be within the jurisdiction of the local police and it was Crocker who was allotted the task of investigating it. After his initial enquiries proved fruitless, he decided that the case warranted a discreet plain-clothes visit north of the river to assess the crime scene for himself. Having identified the exact site of the theft and interviewed some passers-by, he was no further along in solving the mystery and thought that he should investigate further by making some enquiries in a nearby hostelry.

Thus, it was that PC Crocker, looking rather like a character from *The Sweeney* or *Starsky and Hutch*, wandered through the portals of the Herald Lounge Bar, removed his sunglasses and ordered a half pint of lager shandy. It was late afternoon; there were half a dozen or so customers in the bar and two middle-aged men in particular attracted his attention. One was a plump, rubicund individual who looked as though he had slept in his cheap suit; the other was a sharply dressed, thin-boned swarthy gentleman who was sporting a great deal of gold jewellery. The table in front of the two men was covered in empty bottles and dirty glasses and as PC Crocker seated himself at a vacant table to collect his thoughts, the plump man shouted to the barman, ''Ere Tom. Two more of them cocktails, whatever they were.'

The barman looked up and without hesitation replied, 'Coming right up, Vinnie.'

'*Mr* Archer to you, son.'

'Sorry, *Mr* Archer.' Suitably chastened, Tom the barman mixed the cocktail and then served up two tall glasses that were full of an opaque fluid in which floated a few scraps of fruit under the shade of a small paper umbrella.

'On the slate, Tom,' slurred the big man.

'No problem, *Mr* Archer.' Tom returned to his post behind the bar.

If PC Crocker had been a better detective he would have recognised the two men as being well-known local gangsters: Vinnie Archer and Kenny Craft, but he did not because he wasn't. What Crocker did realise, however, was that both men were locals and as such might be able to help him in his investigation.

Crocker hesitated only briefly then, whispering to himself, '*Carpe diem*', rose from his chair and crossed the lounge bar to where the two men were seated. 'Excuse me,' he said, looking from one to the other. 'I'm PC Crocker of Clapham Police and I was wondering if I could ask you a few questions with regard to the theft of a bicycle from outside this pub on Wednesday of last week.' Having said his piece, he stood back to await a response. He did not register the rustle of a newspaper from a nearby table or the crash of glass as Tom dropped the tumbler he was drying. He did, however, notice the immediate change in the facial expressions of the two men he had addressed.

'Wot?' The smaller of the two men looked up at Crocker, a stunned expression on his face. 'Are you kidding me, son?'

'No, sir,' replied Crocker, 'I just happened to observe that you two are regulars here and thought that you might be able to help me in my enquiries.'

'You really a copper?' The swarthy, bejewelled man looked at Crocker, disbelief written all over his face.

'Yes, sir, would you like to see my credentials?'

'Keep your credentials to yourself, son.' The expression on the faces of the two men slowly relaxed and after a knowing glance at one another, both began to chuckle. It was the plump one, Vinnie Archer, who spoke first. 'A bicycle theft, you say?'

'Yes,' replied Crocker. 'Wednesday of last week, approximately 3 pm. Silver frame, drop handlebars and pink mudguards. Quite distinctive, actually.' Crocker sensed that he might be on to a constructive line of enquiry so he reached for the notebook in the pocket of his bomber jacket, withdrew the small pencil from its sleeve on the spine and licked the tip ready for action.

If Mr Vinnie – the Bowman – Archer and Mr Kenny – the Giant – Craft had not been drinking heavily for the best part of 24 hours, their response would likely have been more guarded and the outcome of this episode could have been unrecognisably different. But they had been and were, in the vernacular, well-oiled and totally wellied. In addition, they had been completely wrong-footed by this blundering plod who genuinely did not seem to have any idea whom they were. The two criminals had known each other since leaving school and generally got on well together despite being in competition. Vinnie's territory was North London; whereas Kenny the Giant largely worked south of the river. Both had been arrested on numerous occasions but the police had never garnered sufficient evidence to sustain a conviction and, to the frustration of the authorities, they had always walked free. Thus, they existed in that crepuscular world on the criminal fringe of society: free men for the moment but constantly under the threat of arrest by the police and maintaining a fragile balance of power with other factions of their own fraternity with a delicate mix of violence and bluff.

Kenny Craft stroked his chin thoughtfully. 'Bike theft you say? Nasty business.' He looked up at Crocker, 'Anyone killed?'

Crocker looked up, surprised by the question. 'Not that I'm aware of.'

'Ah, that makes it petty crime then. You'd best speak to my colleague here. He's an expert on petty crime. Stealing old ladies' handbags, that sort of thing. I think he parked on a double yellow line once.' Kenny then slapped his hands on his knees, burst into roars of laughter and, with tears of mirth running down his face, slumped back into his seat.

Crocker, pencil still poised above his notepad, turned to Vinnie Archer whose face was suffused with rage as he stared at his friend. '*Petty*? Me petty?' he blustered, '*I'll* tell you petty. Who was it who did the 'ackney Barclays job then? Tell me that. *Me.* That's who. Over an 'undred thou, that was.' Archer crossed his arms, sat back in his chair and continued to stare malevolently at Kenny.

Kenny the Giant slammed the table with his fist, making Crocker wince.

''Undred thou! Not worth getting out of bed for. Small fry. That's what you are, Vinnie – small fry. You should be called Vinnie – *Small Fry* – Archer. That's wot.'

'You better watch wot you're saying, Kenny, you're beginning to annoy me.'

The Giant's voice rose in pitch and volume. 'If you want proper crime, then who d'you think did them post office vans last summer? *Me*, that's who. Two mill' that was. Now that's wot I call a heist, not your petty few quid.'

During this interchange, Archer and Craft seemed to have completely forgotten the presence of Crocker who was becoming ever more bemused by the direction the conversation had taken. His mouth half open and his pencil poised, Crocker looked from one to the other as the two men traded insults. All he had wanted was some information about a stolen bicycle and here were two drunks trading insults and trying to outdo one another on the magnitude of their past misdemeanours. Suddenly, both men registered that Crocker was staring at them wide-eyed and realised how compromising their tirade had been. For a fraction of a second, there was complete silence in the bar, and then pandemonium broke loose.

The two men who were seated nearby and had appeared to be reading newspapers leapt to their feet, knocking their table over as they did so and raced to where Vinnie and Kenny were seated. As they approached, Crocker saw to his horror that each of them now held a pistol.

'Armed police! Don't move a muscle. Hands in the air!' one of them yelled, pointing his gun at Kenny.

As Archer and Craft slowly lifted their hands in the traditional gesture of surrender, one of the armed men turned to Crocker. 'You too,' he said. On hearing this, Crocker threw up his arms as far as he could, dropping his pencil and notebook in the process.

The two gangsters had rapidly sobered up and now realised that they were the targets of a sting operation.

Crocker himself was totally confused. In the space of what seemed a few seconds, the two gangsters were frisked and handcuffed. Then came the scream of sirens and several more men, some in uniform and others in plainclothes, burst into the bar. Crocker, his hands still in the air, mouth open and eyes wide with astonishment, turned and looked vacantly at the armed man who was still pointing his gun at the two restrained criminals.

'You can put your hands down now, Crocker,' said the man holding the gun without taking his eyes off his prisoners.

Crocker then had a complete mental collapse, the first of many that would occur in the next few weeks. His brain just shut down and he simply stood still, grinned inanely and muttered, 'Ugh.'

'Put your bloody arms down,' the man shouted. Crocker let his arms flop to his sides.

'Are you the police?' Crocker asked faintly.

'No. We're Santa Claus and his elves. Sorry we're a bit late for Christmas.' The detective looked coldly at the bemused Crocker. 'Of course we're the bloody police. We're the Flying Squad.'

As the two handcuffed men were led from the bar, Craft hissed at Crocker, 'Very clever. Think you're clever, Crocker? Well, I'll get you for this. You're *dead*, mate.'

Unsettled by the events of the last hour or so and by this threat, Crocker rather unsteadily retrieved his notebook and pencil before collapsing on to a seat while a uniformed officer, the braid on the peak of his cap pronouncing him a Chief Superintendent, approached.

'You nearly screwed the whole thing up, Crocker; but lucky for you the Sweeney here, who have been following our chums, Vinnie and Craft, for several days, have taped the whole conversation. We should be able to play one off against the other.'

Crocker was absolutely stunned. 'Ugh,' was all he could utter. As the senior officer turned to leave, Crocker suddenly remembered his mission. 'Excuse me, sir,' he called to the retreating figure. The policeman turned, 'Yes, Crocker?'

'You don't happen to have seen a drop-handle bicycle, have you? Silver with pink mudguards?'

The Chief Superintendent shook his head in total disbelief, then turned and left the bar without replying.

It was Craft the police most wanted for the post office job; while Archer, in return for being granted immunity from prosecution for his own misdemeanours, turned Queen's evidence. So after a long and well-publicised trial, Kenny the Giant Craft was sentenced to ten years behind bars.

Chapter 3

'Fancy going to the pub tonight, Lucy?' Andy lay stretched out on the sofa in the sitting room, a lit cigarette in one hand, an open paperback in the other. He could see Lucy, who was busy in the kitchen, through the open serving hatch.

'Thanks, Andy, but I've got a date.'

Andy stubbed his cigarette out in the overflowing ashtray on the floor beside him. 'Oh! Who is it this time?'

'A guy called Nigel.' The fridge door slammed. 'Want a coffee?'

'Yes please. Who's Nigel?'

Lucy came in with two mugs of coffee and handed one to Andy. 'Fifteen sugars, is that all right?'

'If that's all there is.' Andy slurped noisily from his mug. 'So who is this Nigel? Is he the latest in the long line of Lucy conquests?'

Lucy settled herself into an armchair and took a sip of her drink. 'Nigel Bernard-Fielding, ackshully.' Her cheeks dimpled as she giggled.

'Nigel Bernard-Fielding. He sounds like a complete twat.'

'He's the new lawyer at work. I told you, he's really 'andsome. Anyway, he started chatting me up and yesterday asked if I wanted to go to a show with 'im. Said 'e's got some tickets for a concert.'

'What sort of concert?'

'No idea. Think it's opera or something like that. To be 'onest, I wasn't listening. I 'esitated just long enough to make him realise that I wasn't a complete pushover and then said, "Yes".'

'Bet it's a load of rubbish.'

'You're just jealous, Andy Norris. He's really nice. Anyway, you can make your own mind up: 'e's coming round in about an hour to pick me up. I'm off to get ready.'

Just under an hour later, Lucy came downstairs in a cloud of heady perfume. She joined Andy in the sitting room where he had remained in his supine posture on the settee. Lucy was a pretty girl in a straightforward sort of way. East End through and through, her hairstyle was a copy of that made fashionable by Olivia Newton-John, shoulder-length but layered down the sides and back. Her low-cut, patterned blouse was drawn in under the bust, emphasising her ample breasts and showing a seductive décolletage. Her miniskirt exposed most of her thighs while her height was enhanced by a pair of shoes with six-inch stiletto heels bought especially for the occasion. Her outfit was pretty but not elegant and did her figure no favours, making her look rather plumper and more rounded than she was. Her fashion statement was clear: I'm a pretty, working-class girl with no pretensions who likes to dress up and have a good time.

'How d'you think I look?' she asked, twirling round in front of where Andy was lying.

Andy looked her up and down. 'I think you look great. Sure you wouldn't rather come to the pub with me instead of the opera with Nigel Twatfeatures?'

'Don't you be rude to 'im.'

At that moment, the doorbell rang. 'There 'e is now,' said Lucy as she ran to answer the door and a moment later, a good-looking young man dressed in a suit with a beige mackintosh over his arm was ushered in. Andy put his book down, swung his legs to the floor and stood up to welcome Lucy's date.

Lucy stepped forward and with obvious pride announced: 'Andy, I'd like you to meet Nigel Bernard-Fielding.' She then stood aside, her arms wide open as though she had just introduced a Music Hall act.

'Call me Nigel,' said the visitor while pumping Andy's hand vigorously.

'Why?' replied Andy who then, seeing the confusion on Nigel's face and annoyance on Lucy's, immediately added, 'Of course, Nigel, I'm Andy, Lucy's housemate.' Andy assessed Lucy's date. He was just short of six feet, handsome with regular features, had short neatly combed black hair and Andy was sure he could detect a faint smell of Brut aftershave. Nigel was polite and had a firm handshake but there was something about his manner that Andy did not like. He could not quite put his finger on what it was but somehow he was uneasy about this man. He was too perfect: his face too symmetrical, his hair just a shade too dark, his parting unnaturally straight. All in all, slightly too good to be true. 'Would you like a beer?' asked Andy.

'No thanks, Andy, old chap. Brought the wheels along tonight. I never drink and drive.'

'Very wise.'

'Nigel's got an MG Midget,' announced Lucy, touching his arm. 'Haven't you, Nigel?' she added as though he might have forgotten what type of car he owned.

'Yes, managed to get seventy out of her last week, then had to throw out the anchors when I saw a police car in the opposite lane.' Nigel made a snorting sound, the nearest he ever came to actually laughing.

Andy bit his tongue and said, 'Oh good.'

'What type of velocipede do you drive, Andy?' asked Nigel.

'None. Lost my licence.'

'Oh I say, bad luck. How was that?'

'Drinking and driving. Well over the limit: the breathalyser exploded.'

'I'm very careful about how much I drink. In my job, it's essential to stay mentally in top form.'

'I find that as well,' said Andy who then emptied his can of beer, noisily scrunched it in his hand before lobbing it into the corner of the room in the general direction of a waste-paper basket, where it joined several others along with yesterday's fish and chips wrapper.

'Well, Lucy, old girl, we need to get going. Even in the MG, it will take a while to get into town.' Nigel turned to go before adding, 'Nice to meet you, Andy.'

As she followed her date along the hall, Lucy turned to Andy and smiled.

After Nigel and Lucy had left, Andy switched on the television and settled himself back on the settee to watch the news. He opened another can of beer, lit an Embassy Special and wondered for a while what it was about Nigel that he did not like. 'He's a twat,' he said to himself as Richard Baker, the newscaster, informed the nation that power cuts would continue and that a convicted criminal had escaped from custody. It was then that the lights went out.

***

To say that Crocker had been unsettled by the events in the Herald Lounge Bar would be an understatement. His uncomplicated, neatly compartmentalised life had been thrown into turmoil. He had gone to investigate a missing bicycle and ended up being an integral part of the capture of two well-known gangsters. He had later learned that members of the Flying Squad, his heroes, had being tailing Archer and Craft for several weeks as intelligence had led them to believe that they might be planning a joint operation. However, on this particular occasion, the two gangsters had not met to discuss business at all and the officers of the Sweeney had found themselves following Craft and Archer from pub to pub as they went on a massive bender. As well as having to change personnel regularly to avoid detection, they found themselves drinking gallons of soft drinks and spending a disproportionate amount of time in the toilet. The two members of the surveillance team, who had followed the gangsters into the Herald Lounge Bar and discretely set up their recording device before ordering yet another grapefruit juice and lemonade, were beginning to think that the operation was a complete washout.

That was when a weedy-looking, prematurely balding young man clad in a bomber jacket blundered over to the gangsters, introduced himself as PC Crocker and asked them if they knew anything about a stolen bike. Both officers were instantly alert. They knew that Craft, in particular, could be violent and it was quite possible that this unwelcome intrusion by a member of Her Majesty's Constabulary might result in Crocker being at the wrong end of a considerable degree of unpleasantness. Such a circumstance would place the officers in a difficult situation because if they went to his aid, their cover would be blown and if they did not, a member of the London Met might be at the receiving end of some serious physical damage, which in all honesty is what they thought he richly deserved.

Luckily, they did not have to resolve this moral dilemma as to their amazement, the two criminals began to attempt to outdo one another with regard to their past misdeeds. It was only when it began to dawn on Archer and Craft that they had been less than discrete that the officers of the Flying Squad, realising that Crocker was now in real and present danger of his life, kicked the table over, raised their guns and arrested the two crooks.

The tape recording of the gangster's conversation was not in itself adequate evidence to convict both criminals. However, it was enough to persuade Archer that it would be in his best interest to shop Craft in exchange for immunity from prosecution. It was Craft, the more dangerous criminal of the two, the police most wanted inside. Not only was the post office van heist the biggest haul since the Great Train Robbery, but the two drivers had been hospitalised for several months. Craft's own assessment had been correct: he was a violent gangster whereas Archer was essentially just a jumped-up petty thief.

Archer, though, was not stupid. He knew that Craft would want revenge; however, he had calculated that with Craft out of commission, the revenue resulting from the increased business opportunities would allow him to retire abroad, safely hidden, long before Kenny the Giant was released.

After the arrests and during the trial, Crocker had been concerned for his own safety. However, as time passed and Kenny Craft was sentenced, Crocker was reassured by his superiors that on his release, Craft's vitriol would be directed towards Archer rather than himself and Crocker settled back into his uninspiring life. The little unpleasantness in the Herald Lounge Bar had made Crocker realise that he was not cut out for an exciting, adrenaline-charged, danger-filled life and had banished, once and for all, his ambition to join the Flying Squad. The very day after the arrests, he had taken his bomber jacket to the Salvation Army shop and donated it to the homeless. His brief, unintentional exposure to undercover police work had demonstrated beyond all possible doubt that he was far more at home with missing dogs and lost property than organised crime with its attendant gangsters and firearms. There was a dangerous world out there that Crocker no longer wished to be part of. Besides, there was still the case of the stolen bike to solve.

The first that PC Crocker knew of Kenny Craft's escape was when he heard it on the nine o'clock news. Well, he actually heard half of the story. Richard Baker had just finished reporting that power cuts would continue and how Edward Heath would not give in to the miners' demands when he began a news flash about how Kenny Craft, a convicted gangster, had escaped from custody. It was then that the television shut down and the lights went out. Crocker now realised that the game had changed. Somehow Craft had escaped and would now be looking for retribution: there could be no doubt that in his sights would be PC Crocker along with one Vinnie the Bowman Archer.

Crocker started to panic. His heart raced and, if the lights had not gone out, an observer would have noticed how pale and sweaty he had become. He recalled how, after he had been arrested, Kenny had threatened to kill him. He had no idea when Craft had escaped but it was likely to have been more than 24 hours ago and Crocker realised that Kenny Craft was probably stalking him under cover of the blackout furnished courtesy of the striking miners. His hands shook as he reached for the box of matches that he had prepared for this very exigency and he felt faint as he groped his way across the room to the coffee table where a candle stood ready in an empty jam jar. As he attempted to open the box of matches, his fingers trembled even further. He fumbled and dropped the box and its contents spilled out on to the floor. It was pitch black in his sitting room and as he scrabbled on the carpet trying to locate the matches, he heard the hall door ominously squeak open.

Chapter 4

Kenny Craft could not believe his luck. The power cut could not have been timed more perfectly if he had thrown the switch himself. At the very moment that he had stepped from the Black Maria on to the tarmac of the prison yard in front of the main entrance to Her Majesty's Prison, Wormwood Scrubs, the huge arc lamps that lit the area dimmed and were then extinguished, leaving it in stygian blackness. This is where Kenny's size, or rather lack of it, came into its own. One of the two escorts had released his arm in order to close the back door of the van and as darkness descended, Kenny seized his chance. Twisting and turning, he aimed a well-executed kick to the second warder's shin resulting in him loosening his grip just enough for Kenny to break free and slide to the ground. The two officers, sightless in the sudden darkness, punched and grabbed at the space where a man of average height would have stood. One of them caught hold of a torso and managed to place an arm lock around what he thought was Kenny's neck, only to be informed, in no uncertain terms, that it was his colleague that he was attempting to strangle.

Kenny meanwhile crawled at ground level towards the gate. As luck would have it, the electric gates had stopped closing just before they were completely shut. The gap was small but there remained enough space for Kenny to squeeze through. Had he been any larger, he would not have managed it but he was not and he did; so a few minutes later, he found himself, handcuffed but free, in the darkness of Ducane Road. By the time the prison's generator had kicked in and relit the yard, Kenny was already next door within the grounds of the Hammersmith Hospital where emergency generators lit up the campus. Kenny ran to some outbuildings and entered the laundry, which seemed to be deserted. Inside, he located a cloakroom where he spread soap from the dispensers over his forearms and hands. Like the rest of him, his wrists were very thin and eventually with much painful tugging, considerable discomfort and some inelegant language, he slipped off his handcuffs. Searching in a dirty laundry bag, he discovered a suit of clothes into which he quickly changed.

Newly attired in an eccentric combination of garments, which incorporated a striped pyjama jacket, an operation gown and a surgeon's green trousers all of which had a strong odour of urine, Kenny strode purposefully towards the exit holding the handcuffs in his hand. While he was still a few yards away, the door was suddenly kicked open and a hefty woman walked in, her sleeves rolled up to reveal the arms of a pugilist. 'Ere, who are you?' she asked, her eyes narrowing with suspicion.

'Night staff, missus,' replied Kenny without hesitation. Then on seeing the woman looking quizzically at the handcuffs, added, 'Amazing what you find in them laundry bags, innit? 'Ancuffs, would you Adam and Eve it? 'Ere you are, you'd better take them,' and without thinking, the startled woman took the proffered cuffs. 'Well, I'm off for my break. See you later.' Kenny smiled at the unintentional pun and whistling quietly, left the laundry building, crossed the hospital grounds and clambered over a fence to enter Wormwood Scrubs Park.

***

Of all those who were watching the nine o'clock news that evening, there could be no doubt that the worst affected was Vinnie the Bowman Archer. He had heard that Kenny had gone down for ten years and although uneasy about the events leading up to his conviction and sentencing, now that his old school pal had been transferred to the Scrubs, he began to breathe more easily. He was seated at the bar in The Plough, a pub in his own patch in North London, when the news broke. As the face of Richard Baker, who had announced his escape, faded from the screen, darkness descended in the lounge bar. Then suddenly a buzz of conversation broke out. Faceless voices from the gloom muttered and complained.

The landlord was the first. 'Oh bloody hell, not again. 'Ang on, I'll get the candles.'

'Them bloody miners.'

'Wonder how long they'll be out this time?'

'What, the miners?'

'Nah, the lights, you idiot.' the speaker chuckled.

Then, as the bar was gradually illuminated with flickering candlelight, a bonhomie developed as drinkers, who only moments before would never have dreamt of talking to anyone else in the bar, threw down their newspapers and moaned about the common enemy.

'Reminds me of the blackout,' said one aged voice.

'Yeah, this is nothing compared to the blitz, son,' came a faceless reply.

'If you think this is bad, mate, you should 'ave been 'ere in forty-one.'

'Tell me about it. Now that was a *real* crisis, that was.' Voice number one stopped and there was a slurping sound as he took a deep draught from his pint mug before continuing, 'Bomb landed just up the street, outside old Mrs Jones' house it was. Lucky to survive – me. Poor Bernie got it. Took days to find 'im in the rubble. Had 'is head blown off, 'e 'ad.'

'Yeah. I remember him. Owed me ten bob, 'e did.'

A new voice, younger sounding, joined the conversation. 'Look, gentlemen, this is the seventies and we're not at war. It's totally unacceptable that a group of miners are holding the country to ransom.'

The man who was lucky to be alive responded, 'You tried doing their job, mate?'

'Well, no.'

'What *do* you do then?'

'I'm a student.'

'Well then, it's none of your business, is it?' said the man who was owed ten bob.

'Bloody students,' replied the lucky-to-be-alive man.

''Ere, who wants a beer? How about you, student boy?'

And so the discussion continued until three quarters of an hour later when the lights flickered back on and the conversation stopped as abruptly as it had begun. Candles were extinguished, newspapers lifted, reading resumed and the intimacy engendered by a shared adversity evaporated like wispy clouds on a hot summer's day. That is, until someone noticed a body on the floor.

'*Bloody hell*,' cried the man who was owed money by the headless victim of the blitz. '*Bloody hell*,' he repeated. ''e's dead!'

There, lying prostrate on the floor, as he had been since he had fallen off his bar stool the moment the lights went out, was Vinnie, stone dead from a massive heart attack.

***

'Is there a Mrs Zeph, Zeph?' Andy did not look up from his copy of the *Evening Standard* as he asked this of the man sitting opposite him at their usual table in the Herald Lounge Bar.

'Several, man.' Zephaniah circled the name of a horse running in the 2.30 at Newmarket with his red crayon. He was wearing an ancient black leather jacket and perched on the back of his head was what he referred to as his lucky hat, which was an old tweed peaked cap.

Andy looked up. 'Several?'

'Yeah.'

Andy lowered his newspaper. 'How can there be several Mrs Zephaniah's?'

The big Jamaican put his copy of the *Racing Times* down on the table with a sigh. 'Look, man. I is trying to concentrate here. If these horses don' win, it'll be your fault for ruinin' my train of thought.'

'Sorry, Zeph, but I'm just interested to know how you've managed to acquire several Mrs Zephaniahs when I haven't got any.' Andy looked at the ceiling, a puzzled yet vacuous expression on his plump face. Then, realising the implication of what he had just said, added, 'Not Mrs Zephaniahs, obviously. I mean Mrs Norrises.'

Zeph laid his crayon down, carefully marking his place in the running order and gazed at Andy with a look of resignation on his face. 'Well, there's me mum to start with. She's back in Jamaica—'

Andy interrupted, 'No, I didn't mean your mum; everyone's got one of those.'

Zephaniah continued undeterred, '...Then there's me gran, not that she's got long to go—'

'No, Zeph, no. I didn't mean them, I meant *wives*.'

'Oh, man, why din' you say so? In that case, just the two.'

'Two?'

'Yeah, two. But that's not counting Rosie.' Zeph was thoughtful. 'But that was years ago. We was never properly married, so she don' count.'

'So how many have you got now?'

'I told you, just the two.'

'How d'you manage that? As I understand it, you're only allowed one. Well, one at a time.'

'Not in Jamaica, you're not.'

'Bloody hell. How can you afford them?'

Zephaniah's face took on a knowledgeable expression and he pointed his index finger at Andy's chest. 'The question you have to ask yourself, ma man, is how can you afford *not* to have them?'

'What d'you mean?'

'Well, man, they pay for stuff. You know – food, clothes – that sort of thing. If you only have one wife, they can only pay for so much.' Zephaniah paused for a moment and held his hands close together to indicate a small amount. 'But with two wives, you get twice as much,' he then moved his hands further apart before adding, 'but the clever thing is that the costs don't go up two times, more like one an' a bit.' Zeph brought his hands closer together again. 'It makes good economic sense, man.'

Andy shook his head, rose from his seat and wandered over to the jukebox. A moment later, the Carpenters could be heard warbling that they were *On Top of the World*. Back at the table, Andy continued the theme, 'But how do you, well, you know, live together?'

'How you mean, man?'

'Conjugal rights, *you* know.'

'Conjugal whats?' Zeph, who had resumed choosing his horses, looked up, a puzzled expression on his face.

'You know – *sex!*' Andy genuinely wanted to know about other people's sex lives as he was convinced he personally was missing out badly. In fact, he knew he was because he did not have one. He had had a few girlfriends over the years but, for reasons he could not quite understand, they never lasted more than a few weeks. He had begun to think that it might be something to do with his lifestyle.

'Oh! That, man, I leave that up to them.'

'Oh. Are there any little Zephs?'

'Yeah, man.'

'I think I might regret asking this, Zeph, but how many are there?'

Zephaniah put his paper down once more, looked up at the ceiling and concentrated. 'Well, let's see,' he said. 'There's Jo: he's the eldest – his mum's back in Jamaica. Then there's the twins, Elvis and Aaron.' Zeph paused for a moment and looked at Andy. 'That was his name you know. Elvis Aaron Presley. It's my personal tribute to the King. They're ten now. Then there's the girl, what's her name? Ah, man, I always forget her name.' Zephaniah screwed up his face with concentration. 'Yeah, Sophie. That's it. Then there's Zack and Josie. I think that's all.' Zeph looked at Andy. 'How many was that?'

'Well I began to lose count after four but I think it was six in all.'

'Six. Yeah, that sounds about right. At least it was last time I checked.'

'That's quite a good score, particularly as you work nights.'

'It's inflation.'

Andy had been sipping his beer as Zephaniah spoke and started to choke as he heard this casual comment. When he had stopped coughing, he looked at his friend. 'What?' he said puzzled.

'Inflation, man. I read about it. It's running at 17.5%. That's why we're gettin' lots more babies.'

'Zeph, you're barking mad. Anyway, inflation or not, it's your round, mate.'

'Look, Andy. I've just told you, I've got several wives and six children to feed; I can't afford to buy you drinks. You is single, man, you buy the drinks. Why d'you think I come in here and sit next to you? It's not 'cos I like you – you is white trash – it's because you buy the drinks, man.' Zeph's face creased, he threw his head back and cracked up with laughter. A deep, throaty roar of laughter. 'Just jokin', ma man. Same again?'

'Yeah. Thanks Zeph.' As Zephaniah strolled to the bar to replenish their drinks, Andy topped up the jukebox and Leo Sayer wailed out tinnily that the *show must go on.*

On his way home that night, Andy decided that he would ask Lucy out. Properly, not just a casual, 'D'you want to go to the pub?' but a proper date. *It would need to be something special to compete with Nigel Twatface,* thought Andy, *maybe a darts match. The match against the Horse and Hounds' first team would be a good one,* he thought, as he made his habitual stop at the North Sea Fish Bar and wandered unsteadily back to Parkview.

Chapter 5

Kenny the Giant Craft was lucky, very lucky. He had heard the dogs and police search parties shouting in the distance but the power cut had lasted just long enough for him to escape from the immediate vicinity of the Scrubs and now, after a couple of cold nights sleeping rough, he had reached the sanctuary of his safe house.

His overwhelming desire was to seek immediate retribution from Archer but he knew he had to be careful as the police would be anticipating that and watching the man who had stitched him up. Then there was that plodder Crocker. 'Clever trick, that,' he said to himself as he gazed out of the window at the small backyard below. 'You've got to give him credit. Brave too. For Crocker to do what he did took balls, lots of them. Well, two anyway.' Kenny turned and sat down on the single armchair in the sparsely furnished flat. 'To pretend to be a complete cretin investigating a bike theft and inveigle what, to all intents and purposes, was a confession wrung out of me and Archer in the presence of the Sweeney was clever – very clever. You've got to respect a copper like that.' His mind wandered as he recalled the circumstances of his arrest. 'Dangerous, too. I should 'ave known. You could see it in his eyes. It was there, that faraway look. Cunning and dangerous – that's Crocker. Mind you, he disguised it well. There's no doubt he looked like a complete idiot. Anyhows, I'll get 'im; but first there's Archer. He'll be shitting himself now he knows I'm out.'

Craft was shaken out of his reverie by a knock at the door of the flat. He had set up this safe house, which was actually a third-floor flat near Clapham Junction, years ago for just such an exigency as this. Only two others knew of its existence: one was Vinnie, who was hardly likely to come calling, the other was myopic Mick, the assassin. Kenny was scared of very few people. He took care to make sure that others were more scared of him but Mick frightened him. He was dangerous, violent and (most worryingly) totally unpredictable. He was reputed to have at least two gangland killings to his name. The only reason that Kenny tolerated him and had availed himself of his services from time to time was that he reckoned it was better to have a man like that on *his* side rather than working for anyone else.

There came another knock at the door. 'Who is it?' shouted Kenny as he reached into a dressing table drawer and withdrew a revolver.

'Open the door, Kenny.' Mick's voice was soft and menacing. ''Old on, son.' Kenny peered through the spyhole in the door, released several chains, then unlocked and opened it.

Outside on the landing stood a slim man who looked to be in his sixties. His face was gaunt and lined while his hands were thrust suspiciously deep into the pockets of a long, brown leather coat, which reached nearly to his ankles. A belt was tied tightly at his waist and the collar of his coat was pulled up around his neck. On his head, he wore a black, wide-brimmed fedora, below which what was visible of his face was dominated by a large pair of thick-lensed spectacles, the type that make the eyes of the wearer look massive as though they were being viewed through a magnifying glass. As Kenny stepped aside to let him enter the flat, the Irishman did not smile or acknowledge him in any way but simply walked past and sat down in the one armchair as Kenny relocked the door.

'Thought you might need my services, Kenny. D'you know what I mean?' Myopic Mick spoke slowly and softly, his gaze never wavering from a small picture of the Virgin Mary stuck to the wall with Blu Tack.

'Yeah, Mick. I'll be 'oled up 'ere for a while until the heat dies down a bit. I need your help, mate.'

Mick said nothing but continued to gaze at the picture.

'First, I need some supplies. 'Ere, I've made a list.' Mick ignored Kenny's proffered hand in which was a folded sheet of paper, so Kenny laid it on the table. 'Then, Mick, I need you to deal with someone for me.'

Kenny looked at Mick, waiting for a response. 'Nice picture,' was all he said. 'She your wife?'

Kenny glanced at the wall. 'No, Mick, that's the Virgin Mary.'

'Ah! Nice-looking woman.'

'Mick, did you hear me? I need you to deal with someone or I'll be the laughing stock of South London. Know wot I mean?'

'That'll be one Mr Vinnie Archer, for sure.'

'Yeah. Him first. Then there's the cop. I need him out of the way as he'll be after me and he's clever, Mick. Very clever. I need to get the message out that no one messes with me and gets away with it. Geddit?'

'For sure, Kenny.' Myopic Mick continued to gaze at the picture then added, 'Vinnie Archer is as good as dead.'

'The fat bastard will be hiding out but someone will know where 'e is. It's your business, Mick, but the Herald Bar might be worth a visit. 'Ere's a grand to be goin' on with.'

Myopic Mick took the proffered envelope, picked up the shopping list and without a further word, headed to the door.

***

When Crocker heard the door of the sitting room squeak open, he knew that was it – he was as good as dead. You don't mess with the likes of Kenny the Giant Craft and get away with it. Retribution was inevitable. He lay on the floor of the sitting room, trying to control his breathing, his heart pounding so fast and loud that he felt it might burst. He heard a soft footfall and knew the end was nigh. Then it happened: he felt a rasping on his cheek and then a warm moist sensation and he knew that he had been stabbed. He was surprised that it had not been more painful and then, in a fit of uncontrollable rage, leapt to his feet screaming, '*You bastard*, where are you, you bastard?' while waving his arms about in a parody of karate moves, thrashing the air and knocking over a small occasional table in the process. This behaviour surprised Barney, his cat, who had just crept into the room and licked Crocker's face hoping for a stroke. As he kicked and punched at the imaginary assailant, Crocker's foot connected with the furry mass that was his cat, which accordingly went sailing across the room. Barney, realising that all was not well with his master, screeched loudly and raced out of the door towards the safety of the airing cupboard, one of his favourite places.

A few moments later, Crocker began to settle down. His eyes had grown accustomed to the dark and he was able to retrieve his matches. His hands shook as he lit the first of several candles and after confirming that there was no one else in the room, he cautiously felt his cheek. Having ascertained to his own satisfaction that he was not haemorrhaging to death, he slumped into an armchair and said out loud, 'Careful, Crocker, old son, you nearly overreacted then. Remember your training.'

Next morning, after a very restless night, PC Crocker was called into the Chief Superintendent's office immediately on his arrival at Clapham Police Station. He had not spoken to his senior since the arrests in the Herald Lounge Bar several months before. The Chief Super was sitting in a swivel chair, his elbows on a large desk in front of him and the tips of his fingers placed together. He was the officer who had instigated the surveillance of the two gangsters since one of them, Kenny Craft, operated on his patch. He had been irritated that one of his most junior officers had unknowingly sprung the trap, which, while resulting in the conviction of Kenny Craft, had detracted from his own contribution to the affair.

'Take a seat, Crocker,' said the Chief Super, waving his arm towards a spindly chair on the opposite side of his desk.

'Thank you, sir.'

'You don't look so good, Crocker, if you don't mind me saying so. Bowels regular?'

'Yes, thank you, sir.'

'Sleeping okay?'

'Well, actually, the cat did keep me awake last night,' admitted Crocker.

'That must be it then. I'd get an early night tonight if I were you, Crocker.'

'I will. Thank you, sir.'

'Anyway, I didn't get you in here this morning to talk about your bowels and sleeping habits, important though these are. No, Crocker, I brought you in here this morning to talk to you about Kenny Craft.'

Crocker felt himself go cold at the very mention of that name.

'Nasty piece of work, our Kenny.' The Chief Super leant forward in his swivel chair and stared directly at his police constable. 'You probably know by now that he's escaped.'

'Yes, sir, I heard it on the news last night, just before the power cut.'

'Damned power cuts; that's how he managed to escape. Well, we need to recapture him, don't we, Crocker?'

'Yes, sir.'

'He didn't like you much, did he, Crocker?'

'No, sir.'

'And why is that, Crocker?'

'I think it might be because he thought I was accusing him of the theft of a bicycle. Dropped handlebars, silver with pink—'

The Chief Super interrupted. 'No, Crocker. It's because you made him look a prat.'

'Oh.'

'Yes, Crocker, you made him look stupid and were also instrumental in his conviction.'

'Oh dear, sir. I'm sorry about that.'

'Nothing to be sorry about, Crocker. You did society a favour. The problem is that as a result of your involvement in his incarceration, albeit not for as long as was intended, his intention most certainly will be to kill you.'

'Oh dear. That *is* bad, sir.'

'Indeed. But the good news is that he hates Archer more.'

'That's good, sir.'

'Well, yes and no. It's good that he hates Archer more than you, certainly, but the bad news is that Archer's dead. And that's not good news, is it, Crocker?'

PC Crocker was now rapidly losing the thread of the conversation. 'Yes, sir – I mean, no, sir.'

'But luckily for you, Crocker, there is some good news.'

'Oh, good, sir.'

'And the good news is that we have managed to slam an injunction on the press so they cannot inform the great British public of Archer's death for the next 21 days.'

Crocker was now totally lost and was not sure anymore what was good and what was bad news. 'Is that good news, sir?'

'Of course it's good news, Crocker, because that means that Kenny won't know that his ex-friend, the man that banged him up, is dead.' The Chief Super sat back in his chair with a satisfied smile.

Crocker thought he should smile as well. 'Oh, that *is* good news, sir.'

'*But,*' the Chief Super suddenly sat forward and Crocker drew back in alarm. 'The bad news is that he won't find him, will he, Crocker?'

'No, sir.'

'So that's very bad news, isn't it, Crocker?'

'Very, sir.'

'Well, Crocker, what are we going to do about this pretty kettle of fish, eh?'

'Difficult to know what to do for the best, sir.'

'I should say so.' The Chief Super once again settled back in his chair, swivelled it a little to one side and then appeared to address the wall of his office. 'Well, I'll tell you, Crocker. I'll tell you what we're going to do.' He swivelled back to face his PC. 'We're going to find Kenny before he discovers that Archer is dead. That's what we're going to do. That way, we'll catch him before he has the chance to kill you horribly. That's good, isn't it, Crocker?'

'Yes, sir. Very good, sir.'

'Well, that's all, Crocker. Thought you should know that we had all eventualities covered and we have your best interests at heart.'

'That's reassuring, sir.'

'Now, remember: keep all of this under your hat. If Kenny finds out that the Bowman is dead, you're as good as dead too, Crocker. Understand?'

'Completely, sir.'

'Any questions, Crocker?'

Police Constable Crocker was about to give his Chief Superintendent a progress report on the stolen bike case but then thought better of it. 'No sir,' he said, rising to his feet.

'That's all, Crocker. Off you pop.' And as Crocker reached the door, the Chief Super added, 'And remember, mum's the word and keep regular.'

Chapter 6

Andy's discussion with Zephaniah about his wives had started him thinking that he should ask Lucy out on a date. She was a pretty girl and he enjoyed her company. *It's true,* he thought, *that she's not imbued with the finest intellect or the best education and has a startling ability to turn the banal into something of apparent consequence.* However, she was bubbly and fun to be with. Andy also had insight into his own condition and knew full well that he was not the most attractive man in the world and that his personal lifestyle was not what was expected of a successful wooer of the fairer sex. He was the antithesis of Nigel Bernard-Twatface, a man for whom he was developing an ever-deepening dislike.

As the days wore on, Andy became more determined to ask Lucy out on a date but it was to be nearly a week before he could speak to her as, in the intervening time, one or other of them had been out every evening. Lucy was busy socially. She had joined a weight watchers club to try to, *Lose a few pounds,* as she put it. Then she had a myriad of girlfriends, both from work and her schooldays in Wapping. As for Andy; well, he had responsibilities as well. There was Zephaniah to meet at the Herald Lounge

Bar each evening and then there were his darts nights, obligations that could not be shirked, however important the competing demands on his time.

Andy was not a very good darts player and the team only put up with him because of his undoubted ability to be able to score a game long after the rest of his team had lost the mental agility to subtract. He played for a pub in Clapham called the Nell Gwynn, or the Nellie as it was known to all those who drank there. Andy's problem was that after a couple of pints, he could barely hit the board with his darts; but perversely, the more he drank, the more numerate he became and he was always in demand at the chalkboard.

It was the following Thursday evening that Andy found himself alone with Lucy in the sitting room of Parkview Cottage. He was in his habitual supine position on the couch, a can of beer in one hand and a cigarette in the other, watching television when Lucy came in from work. After making a mug of coffee for herself, she settled into an armchair and Andy swung his legs to the floor to face her. He had thought long and hard about what would best constitute a first date. He did not want to overwhelm her and so, after careful consideration, had decided to ask her along to the darts match on the following Saturday. He felt that such a venue would in no way be socially threatening for her and might show him in a positive light: as a merry, convivial, even slightly sporty man. Now that the moment had arrived to ask her, he suddenly felt quite nervous and decided to test the waters first. 'How was the opera, Lucy?' he asked nonchalantly.

Lucy's face lit up with enthusiasm. 'Oh Andy, it was brilliant. It was called Jesus Christ Superstar; a religious theme but full of songs. Well, that's wot opera is, innit? And the people. Well, there were men dressed in dinner suits with dickie bows and women in long dresses. It was fab.'

Andy could barely hide his disappointment. 'Oh! Sounds great,' he said quietly.

'And then afterwards, Nigel took me out for dinner. He said he knew a little bistro down a small side street where the food was wonderful. Apparently, very few people know about it and it's one of London's best-kept secrets, but wouldn't remain so for long. He knew everyone there: the waiters, the barman – just everyone. There were roses on the table and Nigel gave me one. He's ever so posh, Andy. The menu was in some foreign language, French, I think. As I started to look at it, he said to me, "Luce, ol' thing, I think it might be best if I ordered for both of us as I know the chef well. Is that okay with you?" I just sat there and was waited on 'and and foot. Then after dinner, 'e said I was the best secretary he'd ever had and asked me to do some special work with 'im. Some confidential legal stuff.' Lucy gabbled on excitedly for a while longer before falling silent.

Andy had tested the water and discovered that it was cold – no, worse – it had frozen solid. His confidence was shot to pieces as he realised that the appeal of spending an evening watching darts at the Nellie, undoubtedly great though that was, might not measure up to Lucy's newfound expectations. Andy was silent for a moment. 'You seeing him again then?'

'Yeah. 'E's asked me to go away with him this weekend. Some country house where a few of his friends are having a party.'

'Are you going?'

'You bet. Apparently, he'll be doing a bit of shooting but if I don't want to do that, I can stay in the house with the other girls and drink Pimms and stuff.'

'Sounds great.'

Lucy, totally oblivious to Andy's despondency, asked, 'Are you doing anything this weekend, Andy?'

Andy lit another cigarette. '*Me*? Yes. Very busy actually. I'm seeing Zeph on Friday and then I've got an away match at the Bull on Saturday. Should be a cracking game,' he said with an enthusiasm he far from felt.

***

'Zeph, I'm still confused. You've got two Mrs Zephaniahs at home and I'm not sure how it works. What are the sleeping arrangements?' It was Friday evening and Andy, after half a dozen pints, still felt dejected. He realised that he had no reason to be so disconsolate as he had never actually asked Lucy out as such. They had been to the pub together on occasion but that was only when neither of them had anything better to do. If he were to be honest with himself, he had never really taken her very seriously. Certainly she was pretty in an obvious sort of way nor was there any doubt that she was sexually attractive and had a bubbly personality; but she had little in the way of conversation, apart from her weight, ex-boyfriends and work. But having made the decision to ask her out and then finding that she was now, to all intents and purposes, unavailable had made her instantly more desirable.

Andy thought Nigel was a twat. But he asked himself whether or not he was just jealous of him. He was good-looking, polite and clearly knew how to woo a girl. Why then did he have a problem with the man? Andy tried to repress these thoughts as unworthy but he could not help wondering what a man like Nigel: upper-crust, well-heeled and handsome, someone who could choose his girlfriends from among the titled classes, was interested in a working-class girl like Lucy, nice as she was. Nigel was everything that he was not. Andy was not stupid – far from it. He had done very well at school but aspirations at his comprehensive were few and goals were set very low. Thus, instead of staying on to take A levels with a view to going to university, he had left school at sixteen and moved to the local technical college to gain a certificate in computer science.

Andy's current job, although undemanding, paid ridiculously well and his skills were in demand. Employers were beginning to realise that, in order to be competitive, they needed to computerise their businesses but most were ignorant of, and many scared of, the new technology. Firms therefore relied on the Norrises of the world to keep their systems up and running and Andy was undoubtedly good at his job. He thus found himself with money and time on his hands but no real aspirations or ambitions whatsoever. He was happy to drink, play darts and have meaningless discussions with Zeph while occasionally delving into his other interests, which were jazz and the Mayan civilisation and its culture.

'I told you, man, they deal with all that sort of thing. You don' mess with either of the Mrs Zephaniahs, I can tell you.' replied Zephaniah.

'So you just do as you're told.'

'Pretty much, man. Now, are you goin' to get me a drink, or not?'

As Andy wandered slightly unsteadily to the bar, he did not notice the slim, middle-aged man sitting at a table in the corner with his face buried in a newspaper. All that was visible above his open copy of the *Evening Standard* was a black, wide-brimmed fedora.

Myopic Mick, for that's who it was, was amazed. Here, bold as brass, sitting in the Herald Lounge Bar quietly having a beer and chatting to someone whom he assumed must be his minder, was a man whom he recognised as Vinnie Archer. Mick peered at him surreptitiously once more, squinting through his thick lenses. He looked younger than in the pictures of him in the press taken during Kenny Craft's trial, but he was confident that it was Vinnie all right. The tatty suit, unkempt hair, the stomach bulging over his belt and that vacant expression were unmistakable. Of course, Mick's vision was not as good as it used to be and he was not known as Myopic Mick for nothing, but there was no doubt in his mind that the man casually chatting to a big Jamaican was Vinnie the

Bowman Archer. This was going to be easier than he had imagined. *A grand for one evening's work*, thought Mick to himself. *Easy money for sure.* Mick settled himself back into the darkness of his corner, felt the reassuring bulge of the revolver in the pocket of his leather coat, took a sip of his orange juice and pretended to peruse his paper.

Chapter 7

Lucy had taken the afternoon off work in order to prepare for her weekend away with Nigel. She was feeling slightly intimidated by the idea of a country-house party. On the one hand, she was happy that she could hold her own in any company and was outspoken enough to handle any snobbery, but if she were honest with herself, she knew that she was more at home going to the pictures or the local dance hall than mingling with those in a social stratum from which, until now, she had been excluded. Nigel had opened the door to a strange new world. A world where you spoke to waiters in French, an alien culture of cut-glass and mahogany, black ties and evening dresses. Now that she had a fleeting glimpse of this novel environment, she was intrigued yet uncertain whether or not she liked what she saw. She had already broken the shackles that had bound her to her working-class past. Several years ago, she had swapped the docklands of her parents – unemployment and drunkenness, gangs and protection rackets – for the relative calm of Clapham. Here, men wore ties and suits and each house had an inside toilet but now, Nigel had introduced her to a whole new level of sophistication. Although poorly educated, she was naturally intelligent: a streetwise girl who had begun to wonder what Nigel actually saw in her. However, for now, she was happy to go along for the ride and make the most of the experience.

Freshly bathed, perfumed and dressed in a style she thought appropriate for a country-house party, which was essentially what she wore to go dancing but with a cardigan on top, she packed a suitcase with enough clothes for a polar trek and waited for Nigel to arrive. Bang on time at six o'clock, the bell rang and Lucy opened the front door to let him in.

'Luce, ole thing,' Nigel looked her up and down and for just the briefest of moments his smile, his genial façade, dropped only to be restored immediately. 'You look wonderful,' he said.

'Thank you.' Lucy offered up her face for a kiss and puckered her lips in anticipation. Nigel, however, kissed her on both cheeks before looking with some concern at the size of her suitcase. Then, greetings completed, he picked up the case, settled Lucy into his MG – the soft top of which Nigel had taken down – and squeezed her bag into the back. Lucy tied a headscarf under her chin, put on her sunglasses and looking ever so slightly like Audrey Hepburn, she settled back in her seat as Nigel guided his sports car across London.

They headed west along the Thames valley and gradually the grimy suburbs of London were replaced by the patchwork of browns and greens that constitute the Home Counties. Lucy recalled with amazement that, apart from an occasional school trip many years ago, she had never been out of London. The only trees and open land she knew were in the Royal Parks. Here, however, there were rolling fields as far as the eye could see. She tried to share her delight with Nigel but the combination of noise from the wind and the engine meant that conversation was impossible, and so Lucy just settled down to enjoy the scenery. By the time Nigel drove his car down a long gravel drive to an impressive Georgian mansion, just over two hours later, it was dark.

Parked on the apron in front of the house were a dozen or so cars and Nigel drew up alongside an ancient Rover. From inside the house came the sound of music and laughter. Nigel jumped out of his little MG. 'Come along, Luce, we don't want to miss the party, do we?' Then, carrying the bags, he set off briskly towards the short flight of broad stone steps that led to the open front door while Lucy struggled to follow in her six-inch stilettos. Nigel rather timidly entered the house and found himself inside a grand vestibule. He dropped the cases on the floor and looked towards the interior. Ahead of him was a large hallway, at the end of which a grand curving staircase led upwards to the first floor. Several couples were chatting, drinks in hand, while at the other end of the chandelier-lit space, music, chatter and laughter could be heard emanating from large doorways leading off to right and left.

As Nigel and Lucy gazed in awe at the spectacle, an elderly man approached them, walking with a shuffling, slightly broad-based gait. He was wearing baggy, threadbare corduroy trousers; a scruffy Viyella shirt was visible beneath an ancient tweed waistcoat while muddy wellington boots adorned his feet. Nigel thought that he would not look out of place, sitting on a park bench on Clapham Common – a plastic bag beside him and a brown bag containing a bottle of cider in his hand. The man seemed to be a flunky of some sort and when he drew close enough, Nigel said, 'I'm Nigel Bernard-Fielding and this,' he stood aside to acknowledge Lucy's presence, 'is Lucy.' Adding rather unnecessarily, 'We're here for the party.'

The flunky looked closely at them both and without even the hint of a smile, said, 'I'll show you to your quarters.' He then picked up the two suitcases and led the way back through the front door, around the side of the house towards some outbuildings. 'You're in the stable block,' he announced as they approached a dimly-lit cobbled courtyard on the far side of which stood a long low building in a state of considerable disrepair. In the centre was a large arch, wide enough to admit a coach and horses and topped by a clock, its hands indicating that it had stopped working at ten past four sometime in the past. The old man then headed for one of the doors that were situated at regular intervals along the front of the building. On reaching it, he lifted the latch, pushed it open and stood aside to let Nigel and Lucy enter. 'It's not luxurious but you'll find it comfortable enough. Settle in and then come back over. Supper's at nine.'

'Thank you,' said Nigel as he delved in his pocket, found a fifty-pence piece and pressed it into the flunky's hand. With a look of mild surprise, the man turned and headed back to the house where another car had just pulled up.

Nigel, whose spirits had been dampened slightly when he had been ushered out of the main house, led the way. Directly inside, a short hall led to a steep flight of stairs at the top of which was a single, poorly lit room that smelled slightly musty. Nigel pushed the door open and looked around. Inside were two single beds and a wardrobe, while a door to the right of the bedroom opened into a small bathroom. 'What d'you think, Luce?'

'It's a bit cold. Brrr,' she said, rubbing her hands together and looking around at the spartan surroundings.

'You're in the country now, old thing. You'll soon warm up. Let's just drop our things and head back to the party.'

Lucy had been inspecting the latch on the door. 'Nigel, there's no lock!'

'You're not going to get burgled, Luce. We're not in London now. People rarely bother to lock their doors in the country.'

Lucy's initial enthusiasm for the weekend was fast waning, but she was determined to put on a brave face. 'I think it's lovely, Nigel, a bit like camping, you know.'

Then, after a somewhat difficult descent down the stairs in her high heels, Lucy, accompanied by Nigel Bernard-Fielding, strolled back to the main house.

***

It was at about the same time that Lucy and Nigel re-entered the mansion to join the other weekend guests that

Zephaniah announced that it was time for him to go to work and with a breezy, "Bye, my man', headed for the door of the Herald Lounge Bar and on to Global Insurances.

Andy looked at his watch. Mickey Mouse's little hand was at the quarter hour and his big hand pointed to nine. He briefly wondered if Lucy was enjoying herself, then gulped down what was left of his pint, stubbed out his cigarette, folded his newspaper so that it fitted into his pocket and with a wave and a breezy, 'Goodnight', in the general direction of the barman, walked out onto Lombard Street. Andy, never the most observant of people, did not notice the man wearing a long leather coat fold up his newspaper and follow him to Bank Station. He did not see the same man board the southbound Northern Line train a little behind him nor did he see that he followed him to the exit when he alighted at Clapham Common.

Myopic Mick the assassin had to bide his time but he was a patient man. He watched Andy cross the road and enter the North Sea Fish Bar and, his hands thrust deep in his pockets, waited for him in the shadows beside the tube station. He was hoping that the man he believed to be Vinnie Archer was heading for one of the many quiet side streets off Clapham Common South Side and was surprised when his target again crossed the road to the Common and sat down on a park bench alongside a tramp. As Andy opened his package of fish and chips and offered some to the tramp, Mick realised that this was an ideal opportunity. The crowd leaving the tube station had dispersed and as he peered through the thick lenses of his spectacles, Mick could detect no one in the vicinity. This was an opportunity not to be missed. He slipped behind the trunk of an old London plane tree situated on the edge of the Common and after one final check to ensure that he was not being observed, reached into his pocket, withdrew his revolver, which was rolled up in his newspaper, quickly took aim and fired. It was then that the structural integrity of the fish batter changed history and the bullet passed harmlessly behind Andy's head to hit Paddy the tramp fair and square in the temple. Mick, however, did not know this for as soon as he had pulled the trigger, he turned, replaced the pistol in his pocket and walked briskly back to the tube station with the intention of putting as great a distance as possible between himself and the scene of the crime as quickly as he could – as is considered best practice amongst assassins. Back in the Underground, he boarded a northbound train and left the tube at Kennington. There, he hailed a cab and asked the driver to take him to Clapham Junction, thus giving the impression that he was travelling south, towards rather than away from the crime scene. Once there, he paid the driver, gave him a handsome tip and walked by a circuitous route the mile and a half to Kenny's safe house.

Chapter 8

At first, Andy simply failed to grasp what had happened. He froze. His right hand, in which he held the newspaper with its portion of fish and chips, remained extended in a final offering to the dead man, who was now half-sitting, half-lying on the park bench beside him. For some time, Andy could only stare, wide-eyed and unbelieving, his jaw open, a piece of fish half in and half out of his mouth.

Andy was unsure how long he remained thus: unseeing, barely breathing. Then he became aware of someone screaming and he realised it was himself. Andy screamed and screamed and screamed. Taking in great lungfuls of air, he yelled as loudly as he could until he ran out of wind, then inhaled as deeply as possible and repeated the process. No other part of him moved. His eyes remained fixed on the vagrant lolling next to him. Andy's arm remained extended, the open package of fish and chips in his hand. Then Andy moved. He jumped up, threw away the packet containing his supper and proceeded to leap up and down while simultaneously screaming. Suddenly he felt a slap on his face, then another, and his eyes slowly focused on a little old lady standing in front him. He became aware of a misshapen felt hat with a feather hat-pin to one side, grey hair drawn back in a bun and a wrinkled face dominated by a pair of round wire-framed glasses. 'Stop it, son! Stop it!' she was saying and then as she raised her right hand to deliver another slap, Andy stopped screaming and peered vacantly at the old lady.

'There, there, son. You're just upset. Here, sit down.'

Andy's gaze now wandered from the old lady to the vagrant's corpse and back. 'He's dead! There!' Andy pointed at the body of the tramp on the park.

The old lady looked at Paddy, 'Yes, I know, son. He's been shot. From the look of the entry wound, probably by a Beretta 9mm – difficult to be sure though. But that's no reason for you to behave like a baby now, is it?' The old lady helped Andy to sit down on the pavement and it was then that they heard the sirens.

The police car arrived first and men, some in uniform, others not, with at least one of them armed, leapt out. Two of the plain-clothes officers grabbed Andy, pushed his head down and bundled him into the back of the police car.

As the car sped off, the officer next to him continued to hold Andy's head below the level of the window. 'Sorry about this, sir, but in the interests of your own safety, we need to remove you from the scene as expeditiously as possible.'

Andy could only see his shoes. 'What's happened?'

'There's been a shooting.'

'I know. I was there.'

'We need to ask you a few questions.'

It took them only a few minutes, driving at speed with the siren screaming, to reach Clapham Police Station where the officers, now only slightly less unceremoniously, bundled Andy up the steps and through the entrance. As the door banged shut behind the little group, PC Crocker looked up from the desk where he was stationed. The plain-clothes officers ignored him and escorted Andy directly into an interview room. Once inside, the policemen expertly frisked him and placed his personal belongings on the table. Andy looked around the sparsely furnished room. In the centre was a Formica table on which lay a tape recorder and his belongings, while around the table stood three spindly wooden chairs.

One of the policeman indicated that Andy should sit down. 'Sorry about all that, sir, but after a serious incident, we need to remove witnesses, survivors, etc. from the scene of the crime as soon as possible for their own safety. I'm sure you understand.'

Andy simply stared at the policeman, quite dazed by the events of the last half an hour.

'Now, I need to ask you a few questions. Okay, sir?' He took Andy's silence as approbation. 'Right, what's your name, sir?'

'Andy Norris.'

'Address and date of birth, please.' And so it went on until the door opened and the Chief Superintendent entered, accompanied by PC Crocker.

The Chief Super introduced himself, indicated that the two plain-clothes officers could leave and then he and Crocker sat down opposite Andy.

'Now, Mr Norris.'

Andy looked at the clean-cut features of the senior officer. 'Yes?'

'Nasty business – shooting. Have you any idea who might want to kill you?'

Andy's eyes widened with incredulity. 'Kill me? Surely you don't think someone wanted to kill *me*, do you?'

'Have you made any enemies recently, Mr Norris?'

'I don't have any enemies.' Andy thought for a moment. 'Come to think of it, I don't have any friends, either.'

'Have you been involved in any criminal activity recently?'

'No!'

'To your knowledge, have you killed anyone, either deliberately or by accident, in the last twelve months?'

'*No*! Certainly not.'

'Do you habitually carry any lethal weapons?'

'No.'

'Well, what d'you call these?'

The Chief Superintendent picked up a pack of darts from among the objects lying on the table.

'I'd call those darts.'

'Exactly.' The Chief Super leant forward. 'Do you recognise them?'

'Yes, they're *my* darts.'

'Precisely.' The questioner then leant back in his chair, which creaked alarmingly, and looked at the ceiling. 'Now, Mr Norris, I have to ask myself why anyone should be carrying a pack of darts when they are eating fish and chips while sitting on a park bench with a tramp.'

PC Crocker looked at his senior, a puzzled expression on his face. 'Watch and learn,' the Chief Super had said when he had asked Crocker to join him for this interrogation.

'It could be because they were going to a darts match,' suggested Andy helpfully.

'But that's exactly what he would want them to think, isn't it, Mr *Darts Match* Norris, eh!' He turned suddenly to face Andy. 'Why, I ask myself, why would a nice peace-loving person like you be carrying a set of darts?'

'Because I've got a match tomorrow night.'

'That's what they all say. I suppose it's the away match between the Nellie and the Bell.'

'Yes, it is actually.'

'Should be a good game. Now, I'll ask you once more. Have you, knowingly or unknowingly, upset anyone recently? Enough to want you killed, eh?'

'No.'

'Are you sure?'

Andy thought carefully. 'Well, I did make a pass at one of the secretaries last week that wasn't well-received, but I don't think that would normally warrant an assassination attempt, would it?'

'Not under normal circumstances, no, but these are not normal circumstances, are they?' The Chief Super then looked at Crocker who was staring intently at Andy. 'What are you looking at, Crocker.'

'Nothing, sir.'

'Crocker, sometimes I wonder about you.'

'Sorry, sir.'

The Chief turned his attention back to Andy. 'Now, Mr Norris, if this bullet wasn't meant for you, then who do you think it was meant for? Tell me that, Mr Norris.'

'This may seem obvious but could it have been Paddy, the vagrant, who was sitting next to me?'

'Too obvious, too simple, by far.'

'But he was the one who was killed.'

'Mmm. You may have a point there.'

'But then again, who on earth would want to kill a harmless old tramp?' asked Andy.

'Maybe he wasn't a harmless old tramp. Maybe that's just what he wanted us to think, know what I mean?' The Chief Super tapped the side of his nose.

Crocker coughed quietly into his hand. 'Excuse me, sir, but maybe it was just an indiscriminate shooting. Maybe a young thug, intent on killing someone and the vagrant was the first target he saw.'

'Quiet, Crocker.' The Chief Super was thoughtful for a while, then suddenly sat up straight on his chair. 'You know, I just wonder if this is an example of one of those indiscriminate shootings and the tramp just happened to be unlucky. Wrong place, wrong time. Know what I mean?' The policeman looked at Andy knowingly. 'It could have been anyone. On balance, Norris, it seems unlikely that the bullet was meant for you.'

'That's what I said.'

'You can't be too careful, can you, Crocker?'

'No, sir.'

'Well, Norris, I think that's all we can do tonight. You can go now. If you suddenly remember any reason why someone might want to kill you, then please do get in touch. Crocker here will deal with this from now on. He will be the linchpin, the point of contact, the very hub of the operation so to speak. Won't you, Crocker?'

'Yes, sir. Thank you, sir."

'Any questions, Norris?'

Andy thought for a moment. 'May I have my darts back? It's just that I've got that match tomorrow night.'

'Crocker, give Mr Norris his darts back, would you?'

Crocker picked up the pouch containing the darts and handed it to Andy.

'Right. Norris, off you pop and remember. Keep regular.'

'What?'

But the Chief Super was already half way to the door.

The next thing Andy knew was that he was on the street outside the police station. It was after midnight and he was cold and sober. The events of the evening seemed surreal, as if part of a parallel existence. His ordered life had been shattered. Surely someone had not tried to kill him? He was glad of the opportunity of a walk to regain some sort of order to his thoughts and he set off back towards the Common. Half an hour later, Andy passed the scene of the crime and viewed it from the opposite side of the road. The whole area was now cordoned off and, behind the gently fluttering ribbons, forensic officers with tape measures and cameras were minutely examining the ground around the park bench where he had been sitting just three hours earlier. Andy then made his way slowly back to Parkview where he slumped down on the settee, opened a can of beer and lit a cigarette.

Chapter 9

Lucy knew she was out of place. As soon as she and Nigel crossed the drive and entered the mansion, she felt uncomfortable. The house itself somehow made her uneasy. Despite its size, it felt oppressive. Its grandeur was immediately apparent but it was the slight air of decay, almost of neglect, that surprised her. Her parents' place in Wapping was small but it had always been clean and tidy and there was a place for everything.

Nigel led the way into the drawing room, from where came the sound of a piano trio playing Gershwin, very slightly out of tune. There, standing in couples or in small groups were forty or so guests. The men were generally dressed casually in tweed jackets and cavalry twill, while most of the ladies were wearing cocktail dresses. A log fire smouldered in a huge grate within a heavily sculpted marble surround while faded tapestries hung from the walls. A series of three large threadbare oriental rugs covered most of the floor. Furniture was sparse but scattered about were tables in a variety of shapes and sizes while a massive but tatty leather three-piece suite filled the space in the middle of the room below two huge lit chandeliers, hanging from ornate corniced ceiling roses.

The smell of wood smoke was new to Lucy and made her cough involuntarily as Nigel glanced around the room, looking for familiar faces. For a moment, he seemed disconcerted but then with a look almost of relief, he broke into a smile. 'Ah, there's Rodney. Let's go and say hello,' and he led the way across the room to where a man of his own age was standing on his own, nursing a mug of beer and elegantly smoking a cigarette.

'Rodders! Good to see you.' They shook hands. 'This is Lucy, the girl I've told you about.' Nigel stood aside while his friend kissed Lucy on both cheeks: those empty Mayfair kisses that are devoid of any facial contact.

'Rodney and I were at school together,' explained Nigel.

'So why have you been keeping this little beauty all to yourself, Nige, ol' bean?'

'To protect her from unspeakable lounge lizards like you, Rodney.' Both men laughed loudly – too loudly – in an attempt to demonstrate to those around them what a good time they were having.

'By the way, Rodney, where's our host? Must thank him for the invite.'

'What? Oh, the Right Honourable Rupert? He's over there.' Rodney indicated a rather bizarre-looking young man in his early thirties who was standing in the corner of the room talking to the flunky who had taken their cases to the stable block.

'Okay, Rodders, we'll catch you later.'

As Nigel turned to leave, Rodney caught his arm and whispered into his ear, 'I say, ol' chap, when you're finished with the girl, send her over to me. She looks like dynamite.'

'She is. Believe me, she is,' replied Nigel quietly before guiding Lucy across the room in the direction of their host. Rupert was still chatting to the older man and Nigel stood politely aside until there was a lull in the conversation.

Rupert Forsyth turned to Nigel, a polite smile on his rather rubbery face. 'I'm Rupert. Welcome to Warren Towers,' he said slowly with a smile, extending his hand. He was dressed in a dinner suit that had seen better days and the detritus of much feasting was clearly visible on its satin lapels. His face could only be described as having been shuffled. All the bits were there: eyes, lips and there was definitely a nose and ears but they looked as though they had been thrown together randomly without due consideration to matching or symmetry. His hair appeared to have been cut by a lawnmower, being at once both too long in some places and too short in others but it was his eyes that demanded the observer's attention in that they appeared to be on the side of his head and looking in slightly different directions.

Nigel felt slightly ill at ease in the presence of this young man. Although of a strange and rather disconcerting appearance, Rupert somehow exuded quality and breeding. It was not so much what he was wearing, how he looked, or even what he said. It was more the way he wore his clothes and the quiet confidence with which he spoke.

'I just wanted to thank you for the invite,' said Nigel, rather nervously shaking his hand.

'A pleasure, I assure you.' Rupert smiled and looked questioningly at Lucy.

'This is Lucy,' said Nigel.

Rupert tilted his head slightly in the gesture of a small bow and took Lucy's hand briefly. 'You're most welcome, Lucy.' He then turned to Nigel. 'I'm awfully sorry but I'm terrible with names – you are?'

'Nigel. N–Nigel Bernard-Fielding.'

'Ah, yes of course, I remember now. Cambridge, wasn't it?'

Nigel was about to correct his host and explain that he had not been at Cambridge when Rupert turned to the elderly man at his side. 'Let me introduce my father, Lord Forsyth.'

'We've actually met, Rupert. Mr Bernard-Fielding was kind enough to give me a tip for showing him to his room.' There was a hint of a smile on the old man's face.

Rupert threw his head back and laughed. 'Father, I keep saying you really must dress better.' He looked at Lucy, 'Guests are forever mistaking him for the gardener.'

Nigel felt his face flush and was at a complete loss for words. It was Lucy who saved the situation. With a slight curtsey, she shook Lord Forsyth's hand. 'You've got a lovely place here, your Lordship. Must be difficult to keep clean.'

His Lordship smiled. 'Lucy, my dear, how right you are. It's the very devil to keep warm as well.' He turned to his son, 'Now, Rupert, I think it's time for supper.' Rupert turned to a table behind him where there was a large brass oriental gong that he hit loudly several times with his hand. As the buzz of conversation settled, he announced, 'Ladies and gentlemen, supper is served next door.' Then, turning to Nigel, he added, 'It's just a cold collation tonight. We'll have a formal dinner tomorrow before the dance.'

Nigel, still feeling embarrassed by his gaffe, just answered, 'Lovely.'

'Are you coming on the shoot tomorrow morning, Nigel?' Rupert then creased his brow and looked at Nigel with a puzzled expression, 'It *is* Nigel, isn't it?'

'Yes. I'd love to come along but I'm afraid I haven't brought my gun.'

'Good! Good,' said their host absentmindedly. 'We're meeting outside at five. See you then.' Rupert then headed off to speak to another of his guests.

Lucy meanwhile had helped herself to a glass of champagne and was beginning to feel more relaxed after a couple of gulps. 'I didn't know you had a gun, Nigel. Why didn't you bring it along?' she asked as they joined the end of a straggling queue to enter the dining room.

Nigel looked slightly uncomfortable. 'It wouldn't fit in the MG without looking suspicious. Now, Luce, I hope you're hungry. Country-house parties are known for their lavish spreads.'

'Famished. Rather you than me for the shooting. There's no way you'd get me up at five in the morning.'

'Ah, Nigel, I'd like you to meet my sister, Lucinda.' Rodney had joined them in the queue. Nigel shook hands with an attractive woman whom he estimated to be in her mid-thirties. She was dressed simply but expensively in a plum-coloured cocktail dress, her only jewellery being a set of pearls encircling her elegant neck.

Lucinda smiled at Lucy. 'You poor thing.'

Lucy looked at her in surprise. ''ow d'you mean?'

'Being dragged along here to spend your weekend in this draughty old pile miles out in the sticks just so that these appalling adolescents can play with their toys. I'm sure you'd far rather be in a cosy little pub back in London.'

'Oh, Lucinda, that's outrageous,' Rodney looked at Lucy, 'You mustn't take my sister seriously; I think she's got water on the brain.'

'It's absolutely true, darling. Lucy dear, I'm here only because I'm pathologically attracted to Rupert. He's so eligible.'

Lucy smiled as Lucinda looked at Nigel.

'Nigel, are you going to kill some poor defenceless animals tomorrow?'

'Well, yes. Well, no – not really. I'm just going along for a bit of exercise. I forgot to bring my gun.'

'I'm sure Rupert will have a spare one or two.' Lucinda turned her attention to Lucy. 'Lucy dear, while these overgrown schoolboys are playing soldiers and grazing their knees tomorrow, you and I must have a good old chin-wag and say awful things about them behind their backs.'

Lucy smiled broadly. 'Yeah, that would be smashin'.'

'Good, ten o'clock it is, then, in the library.'

After struggling with a leg of pheasant and some cold lamb cutlets, Lucy decided that she was not hungry after all and felt she would lose more weight here in one weekend than after a month's meetings of weight watchers. She was also slightly surprised that Nigel did not seem to be better known. Apart from that awful man, Rodney, whose sister Lucinda she had immediately taken to, he did not seem to know anyone else. Then there was that dreadful gaffe when he had mistaken Lord Forsyth, the owner of the estate, for a porter. Nonetheless, Lucy was ever so slightly disappointed when Nigel made no attempt to get into bed with her when they returned to their room at the end of the evening.

Chapter 10

Andy was awakened by bright sunlight streaming into the sitting room. He had fallen asleep on the settee while still mentally wrestling to make some sense of the previous evening's events. Andrew Norris was a logical man. He could understand computer programmes, darts scores, Pythagoras and calculus, but became confused when dealing with human beings. Why should anyone want to kill poor old Paddy? The Chief Superintendent seemed to indicate that the situation might be more complex and that perhaps Paddy was not just a vagrant but part of a complex criminal underground network. However, it struck Andy that in any walk of life, whenever there was uncertainty, conspiracy theories abounded and the Chief Super did seem to be a bit of a prat.

Andy remembered the occasion when a magnetic tape containing customers' details had become corrupted and senior managers immediately accused a rival company of industrial sabotage; that was until Andy recognised the tell-tale signs of a liquid spillage on the tape and one of the secretaries owned up to accidentally tipping her morning coffee onto it. Andy had known Paddy for years. He knew that he spent his year travelling around the country and every now and again visiting relatives in various towns. He spent the summer in Scotland, autumn in southern Ireland and usually wintered in London where it was warmer. Clapham Common was one of his favourite haunts as it offered a pleasant outdoor environment to sit and sleep together with the warmth and protection of the tube station when the weather was inclement.

I think that fellow Crocker was probably right, Andy thought to himself. *It was probably just an indiscriminate killing. Maybe someone who didn't like vagrants: perhaps some right-wing fascist.*

Andy showered, changed and then wandered to the shops at the north end of the Common. He bought himself a newspaper, a pack of Embassy King Size cigarettes, some bacon and a loaf of bread. Back in Parkview, he ate a bacon sandwich as he scanned the newspaper. *There was no mention of the shooting, but it might just make the late edition of the Evening Standard,* he thought.

Crocker meanwhile was troubled. Somehow, he felt that the events of the previous evening must be related to Kenny Craft's escape. But why on earth, he wondered, would Craft want to kill a harmless vagrant. Crocker tried to rationalise his own rather vulnerable position in this complex jigsaw. Craft would want revenge – there could be no doubting that. The fact that it was purely by chance that he, Crocker, had played a pivotal part in Kenny Craft's capture and subsequent conviction was immaterial. Craft believed that Crocker had been central to the operation and had, in effect, cleverly made him confess so that in the eyes of the criminal underworld, he had been made to look ridiculous. *However*, thought Crocker, *so far as Craft was aware, Archer was still alive and surely he would want to settle that score first.*

There had been a public outcry following Kenny Craft's escape. It was open season for leader writers. Headlines like 'Miners help violent gangster escape' and 'Vicious criminal loose as a result of power cuts' had appeared on the front pages of many of the tabloids above a picture of the escaped gangster and so the great London public were on the lookout for him as well as the Met. Surely Craft would not dare to be seen out in the open. *And then*, thought Crocker, *there was Norris*. He seemed somehow familiar; he had that irritating feeling that he had seen him before but could not place when or where it was and, like a word that is on the tip of your tongue, the more he tried to remember, the more unattainable the memory and the more frustrated he became. Lastly, he had made no progress whatsoever with the stolen bike, which had disappointed him. Perhaps someone had changed the mudguards to mislead him. The pink ones certainly were highly distinctive. Crocker's mind whirled with possibilities: with intrigue and theories until his brain became sore with the effort. Crocker sighed; *maybe it was all just a coincidence*, he thought, *as the Chief Super had intimated.*

That evening, Andy was not at his best. His concentration, essential for darts, especially in a crunch away game, was not at its best. Every time there was a sudden noise, he twitched and twice, when the door slammed as he was throwing, he missed the board completely, very nearly causing serious injury to the scorer. The captain of his team decided to substitute him for the safety of all concerned and Andy took up his usual position at the blackboard. Even there, he underperformed on several occasions, miscalculating the finishing double that resulted in the home team winning.

After a while, the captain called him over. 'Andy,' he said, 'what's up, mate? Your scoring's rubbish.'

'Sorry, skip,' replied Andy, 'I'm afraid my concentration's not too good. It's probably because I nearly got shot last night.'

'Pull the other one, mate. 'Ere, Larry, take over on chalks, would you?'

Andy was about to protest but thought better of it. There had been nothing in the press that night and he could not be bothered to argue the toss with his captain. He would discuss it further when the shooting had been reported.

Next day, the story was in most of the Sunday papers. It was not headline news; that was reserved for the ongoing struggle with the miners, the three-day week and Harold Wilson demanding that the country should go to the polls. But in the middle pages of all but one of the papers, there was a short piece on the shooting.

None of the newspapers mentioned Andy's name but some noted that a passer-by was lucky not to have been hurt as well. 'Police are actively pursuing a number of leads.' Andy smiled to himself as he read that, 'Well, that's good to know,' he said out loud to himself, remembering the Chief Super's comments. He would certainly have something to tell Lucy when she returned, that was for sure, and he began to wonder how her weekend was going.

***

Lucy, much to her surprise, was actually beginning to enjoy herself. The previous evening had been difficult. Nigel had clearly been on edge and those to whom she had been introduced had been awful bores. Apart from Rodney's sister, she had nothing in common with any of the other guests. No one had anything interesting to say about dieting, the Top Ten or the latest Oxford Street fashions, and the evening had been punctuated by long embarrassing silences but now here she was, sharing a pot of coffee with Lucinda, whose company she found a delight. Lucinda was so outspoken; there was no subtlety in what she said, just outrageous honesty. Lucy thought she was like a breath of fresh air.

'Now, Lucy dear, what on earth are you doing with that terrible fraud, Nigel?'

''Ow d'you mean – terrible fraud?'

'I'm sure he's a lovely man, Lucy dear, but he's nowhere near good enough for a girl like you. Ah! Here comes our host at last.' As Rupert came over to greet them, Lucinda looked up at him and offered her hand. 'Rupert, darling, why has it taken you so long to come and see me? Do you know my new friend, Lucy?'

Rupert bowed slightly and kissed Lucinda's hand. 'Yes, I had the pleasure of making her acquaintance last night. I do hope you slept well. The stable rooms can be a bit cold.'

'I slept very well, thank you, your Lordship.'

'Please call me Rupert. It's my father who has the title.'

'Rupert, do stop talking to Lucy and pay attention to me. When are you going to ravish me? I've been waiting for far too long.'

'But, Lucinda dear, you're far too good for me, and besides,' Rupert looked up and glanced around him briefly before continuing. 'I think I may well be gay.'

Lucinda frowned at her host. 'Absolute rubbish, Rupert.' She then hesitated for the briefest of moments before adding, 'How long have you been gay?'

Rupert hesitated and looked at the ceiling. 'Oh, about ten minutes, I should say.' He looked at Lucy, then Lucinda and smiled innocently.

'Don't talk such nonsense; I know very well that you're not gay. That little trollop Lady what's-her-name told me. You're just saying that to put me off. You know I'm madly in love with you. We should get married and have lots of babies immediately.'

'Well, Lucinda, you'll have to speak to mother about that. She arranges all that sort of thing.'

'Rupert, are you *really* gay? I'd be most disappointed if you were.'

'No, of course not, Lucinda, I just tell the ladies that so that I can get some peace. I really can't afford to marry.'

'Rubbish! You should marry me. I'll have a word with her ladyship; she'll see sense even if you won't.' Lucinda then turned her gaze to Lucy. 'Lucy, don't you think he's just delicious?'

Lucy looked at Rupert and smiled 'Yeah, 'e's alright, I reckon.'

'Isn't she gorgeous, Rupert? So refreshing compared to those pompous hooray-henrys you invite to these do's of yours.'

'I'm inclined to agree with you, Lucinda. That's why I couldn't bear to lead the shoot this morning and left it up to father.' Rupert took a seat alongside the two women. 'Now, Lucy, do tell me all about yourself.'

It was Lucinda who answered. 'Look! Don't get any ideas about my new best friend. It's me that you love; it's just that you don't know it yet. Besides, she belongs to Nigel someone or other. Apparently, he knows my ghastly brother Rodney. Now tell me, Rupert, how long do we have to wait for our first cocktail? It's nearly midday.'

'Come with me, ladies.' Rupert led the way into the library.

'Look at all of them books,' Lucy exclaimed as she gazed admiringly at the book-lined walls.

'It's such a shame that no one here can read. Isn't that right, Rupert? Anyway, forget the books; Lucy dear, it's the bar we're interested in.'

'Lucinda, you're incorrigible. I don't know why I continue to invite you to my little gatherings.'

'You don't, darling; I just turn up and will continue to do so until you give in and marry me.'

Rupert opened a cupboard to reveal a well-stocked bar. 'Lucinda, I don't want you misleading this charming young lady. Unlike you, she works for a living. Where is it that you work, Lucy?'

Lucy gave the name of the law firm where she was secretary, adding, 'That's where Nigel is a partner.'

'I've not heard of them myself but I'm sure they're very good. The usual, Lucinda?' asked Rupert as he lifted a bottle of Gordon's gin from the cupboard.

'Yes please, Rupert. With lots of ice, please. I still have a slight headache from last night.'

'Too much to drink, no doubt?'

'No, not at all. It was the company that was skull-numbingly boring.'

'And you, Lucy?'

'Ooh. Wot 'ave you got?'

It was Lucinda who answered, 'Join me in a gin and tonic, Lucy dear. It resurrects your taste buds ready for a proper drink, doesn't it, Rupert?'

'So you keep saying.'

Rupert handed them each a large cut-glass tumbler chinking with ice. 'Now, Lucinda, you may not believe this, but I do have other guests to attend to and the shooting party will be back soon.'

'If you must go, Rupert, but don't be long; I'm pining already.'

Rupert smiled fondly at Lucinda and then turned his gaze to Lucy, 'Don't let her mislead you. I'll see you both later.'

After he had left the room, Lucinda turned to Lucy. 'Best catch in the country, Lucy dear. He's the real thing: a fourteenth Earl, absolutely charming, irresistibly ugly *and*,' Lucinda looked at Lucy to reinforce her point, '*and* worth at least two million.'

Lucy's eyes widened, 'Really?'

'Yes, but he's mine, darling.'

An hour or so later, the shooting party returned. It had been raining and after laying a few hare and widgeon on the steps leading up to the mansion, they trampled in with their dirty boots, unslung their guns and removed their sodden coats.

A few moments later, Nigel appeared in the doorway to the library. He was soaked and stood there, a picture of misery, dripping muddy water on to the floor. Lucinda burst out laughing, 'Nigel, you're *soaking*. What on *earth* happened?'

'I fell into a ditch.'

'What on earth did you want to do that for?'

'I didn't mean to, for God's sake.'

Lucy, now quite relaxed after two gin and tonics, smiled at himDid you 'ave a good time, Nigel?'

Nigel looked angrily at Lucy, irritated by her question. 'What d'you think? No! Frankly, bloody awful. Nearly seven hours in the pouring rain. One of the buggers seemed determined to shoot me. He said I was in his line of fire and I mustn't get ahead of the guns or something like that. Anyway, I decided to find somewhere warm and sheltered and it was then that I fell into a dyke.'

Lucy and Lucinda chuckled.

'Well, I'm pleased that you two are amused. It's all right for you, sitting here with your gin and tonics.'

'Yes, Nigel, Lucy and I have had a lovely time. Now, go and get changed before you catch your death.'

'Yes I should, I'll be back shortly.'

Lucy made a move to follow him. 'Leave him, Lucy; he's in an awful grump. He'll be better after a couple of drinks.'

'Are you sure, Lucinda? He seems a bit upset.'

'I told you, Lucy, he's a complete fraud. Boys with toys.' Lucinda headed to the bar, 'Same again, Lucy?'

'Why not? I'm beginning to enjoy myself.'

'Oh, I'm so pleased. I was dreading this weekend. Rodney is such a bore and as for the others, there's not an ounce of testosterone between all of them – believe me, *I* know. Nigel may be different of course, but I've tried all the others and they're hopeless. Just no idea. I have high hopes of Rupert though. Cheers.'

Chapter 11

''Ere, Mick, where was it you said you shot Vinnie?'

'In the head, Kenny.'

'No, no, mate. Whereabouts in town?'

'Oh! Clapham Common, near the station. Why?'

''Cos it says here,' Kenny waved his copy of the *Evening News* in the general direction of Myopic Mick, the assassin, 'that some tramp known as Paddy was shot dead there on Saturday night. *That's* why, mate.'

Kenny Craft was becoming restless. He had been indoors, trapped in his safe house, now for over a week and was developing cabin fever. When Myopic Mick had arrived late Friday night and simply announced, 'Job done,' he had been a bit suspicious as the whole process from finding the target to assassination had taken just four hours. Mick, however, was a pro and Kenny had simply accepted his version of events. Kenny had been eagerly anticipating Sunday headlines along the lines of, *Major Gangland Figure Killed*, or, *Vinnie Archer Cut Down in Gangland Killing*. The underworld would then know that he, Kenny Craft, was back in business and was not to be messed with. However, having scanned several newspapers from cover to cover, all he could find was a small piece on the shooting of a tramp on Clapham Common.

'Give me that!' Mick snatched the newspaper from Kenny's hands, took off his thick spectacles and peered closely at the article, his face just inches from the page. He read the article twice, moving his head to follow the words. Eventually, he looked up and replaced his spectacles.

It was Kenny who spoke first. 'What happened, Mick? Wrong man?'

'I don't understand it, Kenny. I must have missed. Archer must have moved just as I fired.'

'That's great, just brilliant. Now the whole bloody world knows that I'm after Archer and he's been warned as well. Mick, you're a liability. You need some new glasses – that's what you need.'

Mick was silent.

Kenny's voice rose in anger. 'Mick, I said you need some new bloody glasses. D'you hear me?'

'It was just bad luck.'

'*Bad luck*! You killed the wrong bloody man, you Fenian idiot.'

'Don't call me a Fenian, Kenny.' Mick's voice was menacing and Kenny immediately backed down. Anyone who could quite calmly admit that he had just killed the wrong man and say, 'It was just bad luck', commanded respect.

'All right, Mick. I'm just a bit tense, that's all. But you'll need to try again.'

'I'll do it next week. I know his habits now.'

'Don't you think he'll change them as a result of this initial *slight* error?' Kenny's voice was thick with sarcasm. 'D'you think he'll go back to the same park bench with a sign on his head saying, 'Here I am, Mick, have another shot?'

'Of course not, but that's the clever bit. I think he'll expect me to think that and therefore not do it in order to confuse me. No, I think he'll do exactly the same on the assumption that that is the last thing I think he'll do.' Mick looked pensive while Kenny looked confused.

'I'm not sure I quite follow that, Mick.'

'You don't need to. In my job, Kenny, you've got to get inside your enemy's head, read his mind and know his every thought. You have to become that man. That's how you catch a thief.'

'Oh!'

'Now, what d'you want for supper? I'll pop down to the supermarket and get us something nice to eat.'

***

'I know what we'll do, Crocker.'

'What's that, sir?'

The Chief Super looked across his desk at his police constable. 'Well, Crocker, what we're going to do is a reconstruction.'

It would be wrong to say that the investigation into the Clapham Common shooting had progressed slowly because in actual fact, it had not progressed at all. It was, to use a sporting analogy, still firmly on the blocks and there was no sign of the starter. Contrary to what the Chief Superintendent had told reporters, he had no leads to follow whatsoever. The tramp had no suspicious background and Norris was just some local loser.

'We need more witnesses, that's what we need, Crocker. What do we need?'

'More witnesses, sir.'

'Spot on, Crocker. We'll set up a reconstruction exactly a week after the original shooting. We'll get someone to dress up as the tramp.' The Chief Super thought for a moment. 'That'll be you, Crocker. And then we'll need someone to impersonate Norris. Come to think of it, he can play himself. Then we'll interview passers-by.'

'I'm not sure I'm the best person to play the vagrant, sir.'

'Nonsense, Crocker, you're perfect for the part. Just don't wash for the next few days and put on your gardening clothes. What we need is maximum publicity without admitting that we haven't got a clue. Brief the press, Crocker. Tell them that we expect an arrest imminently but are going to stage a reconstruction just to confirm our suspicions. Something like that – that'll fool them. And get on to Norris and ask him to do his public duty and repeat his movements of the night of the shooting *precisely* – from his after-work drinks to his journey home via the fish shop. Got that, Crocker?'

'Yes, sir.'

'Nothing can possibly go wrong. That's all, Crocker. Off you pop.'

'Thank you, sir.'

As Crocker got up to leave, the Chief Super looked over his half-moon spectacles at him. 'Still regular, I hope, Crocker?'

'Absolutely, sir.'

***

The whole of Saturday evening was rather a blur for Lucy. She remembered walking back to the stable block and changing into her evening dress with some difficulty. Nigel, already dressed for dinner, was beginning to sneeze and accused her of being drunk.

At dinner, Lucy found herself sitting next to Rodney, Lucinda's brother. It was soon after the soup course that Rodney, who had clearly peaked a little early, put his hand around her shoulders and slurred, 'Nigel said you're dynamite. If you ever get fed up with him, jus' come and see me, Lucy. I'll show you a good time.' Rodney, whose cerebration was clearly sub-optimal, then wondered if his approach had been too subtle so, after belching loudly, he leered at Lucy in an unfocussed fashion and added, 'D'you know what I mean?'

To say that Lucy was surprised would be an understatement. She could barely believe that this well-bred man, Nigel's friend, was propositioning her. Initially, she was not sure whether or not to respond but as Rodney continued to leer and obviously was expecting a reply, she put her left hand over her décolletage and said more loudly than she had intended, 'Ooh, aren't I the lucky one?' Lucy hoped that this putdown would be the end of the matter but she was wrong. It was during the main course that she felt Rodney's hand on her thigh, pushing her skirt higher up her leg. She reached down and tried to remove it but Rodney continued to grip her thigh even more firmly. She thought of attracting Nigel's attention but he was several places away on the opposite side of the table and in earnest conversation with a girl called Amanda.

Although unused to dinner parties of this nature, Lucy was very experienced in dealing with the unwanted advances of inebriated men and knew that only direct action would be effective. She took her glass, which was full of amber-coloured wine, made to lift it to her lips and then when no one was looking, calmly directed it under the table and poured the entire contents into Rodney's lap. The glasses were large and Lucy was gratified to feel Rodney withdraw his hand immediately. Lucy looked at Rodney triumphantly. 'Nice wine, Rodders, ol' bean, don't you think?' She then very ostentatiously refilled her glass to the brim and took a sip. No one else noticed this interchange but at the end of the meal, Lucy was pleased to see that Rodney was the last to leave the table and went directly to his room, all the time holding a napkin over his groin.

The after-dinner entertainment that evening was a ceilidh. Rupert explained to Lucy that his family had Scottish ancestry and invited her to be his partner in the first dance, which was a Gay Gordons. Thus endorsed by the host and relaxed after the day's drinking, Lucy found herself completely engrossed with the various Scottish dances and it was only some considerable time later that she went in search of Nigel, whom she had not seen since dinner. Eventually, she spied him in the vestibule in a clinch with Amanda. He was nuzzling her neck while at the same time groping her left breast. It was at that moment that Rodney walked rather unsteadily into the vestibule and Lucy noted with satisfaction that he was now wearing a clean, dry pair of trousers. Lucy was calm. Before either of the men had noticed, she retreated quickly to the bar, picked up two glass jugs and filled them with iced water. After taking a large swig of her gin and tonic, she then marched back to the vestibule where Rodney was now sitting next to Nigel and Amanda. She approached the little group with a fixed, rather sardonic smile on her face.

'Oh. Hello, Luce, ol' thing,' said Nigel, withdrawing his arm from Amanda's shoulder while Rodney looked up and grinned inanely at her. The first jug of water Lucy tipped directly into Rodney's lap, fervently hoping that he did not have a third pair of trousers to change into. The contents of the second jug were then poured over Nigel's head. Some splashed on to Amanda's dress. 'Sorry, Amanda,' said Lucy as she stood back to admire her handiwork. It was then that Lucy heard a slow clap from behind her and she turned to see Lucinda, cigarette in her mouth, clapping languidly.

'Oh, well done, Lucy. I've wanted to do that for years!'

***

'How was your weekend?' Andy remained in his supine position as Lucy entered the sitting room late on Sunday morning.

'*Fine.*'

'Didn't expect you till later.'

Lucy remained silent, standing in the doorway.

Andy put his newspaper down. 'Are you all right, Lucy? You sound upset.'

'I said I'm *fine.*'

Andy picked up his paper again and spoke almost under his breath, 'You don't sound fine to me.'

'I said I'm *bloody well fine*, Andy. Don't piss me off.' Lucy's voice had risen in both volume and pitch.

Although not especially sensitive to displays of emotion of this sort, Andy knew when it was wise to keep quiet and that this was one such occasion. Although he knew it would be unwise to show it, Andy was actually quite pleased as the weekend with Twatface had clearly fallen far below expectations.

Lucy stormed out of the room and into the neighbouring kitchen where she clattered about noisily before re-entering a few moments later with a cup of coffee in her hand. She threw herself into the armchair and exclaimed, 'Ugh.' This was more an audible demonstration of despair than a word, and Lucy's 'Ugh' was heartfelt and said it all – in spadefuls. Andy studiously peered at his newspaper, hiding his face while trying desperately not to laugh.

'Ugh.' Lucy repeated, while taking another sip of coffee. '*Well*?' she said, staring at the wall.

Andy looked up. 'Well, what?'

'Well, aren't you going to ask me?"

'Ask you what?'

'How my weekend went.'

'I did, just now, and you said fine.'

'I wasn't ready then.'

'Ready for what?"

'Are you being deliberately annoying, Norris?'

Andy was now becoming decidedly confused, unsure what he should say for the best. He settled for, 'No.'

'Well, ask me then.'

'Okay,' Andy swung his legs to the floor and turned to look directly at his housemate. 'How was your weekend, Lucy?' he asked in a bright enquiring manner.

'It was shite. And you know it was. So why did you ask?'

'Lucy, I'm genuinely sorry,' Andy lied. 'Do you want to tell me about it?'

'*No.*' Then, after blinking at the window for a moment to disguise her tears, Lucy launched into the events of the weekend. As her tale unravelled, Andy had to look at the floor to avoid giggling. By the time she had related how she had thrown iced water over Nigel and Rodney, Andy could control himself no longer and burst into fits of laughter.

'Andy, how *can* you laugh? You're an insensitive bastard.'

'It's brilliant, Lucy. You're a star.'

'Funny, that's just what Lucinda said.' Lucy sniffed for a moment, then began to chuckle until the two of them were doubled up with laughter as Lucy described the highlights of the weekend once more.

'So how did you get home? Did Twatface give you a lift?'

'Not likely! I wouldn't let Twatface within a million miles of me. Lucinda was returning to London and dropped me off in Chelsea where she lives. I walked back from there.'

'Lucy, I'm proud of you. I just wish I'd been there.'

They fell silent for a moment. 'Well, Andy, that's the story of my disastrous weekend. How was yours? Quiet?'

'Yeah, quiet. Had a few pints after work, then there was the darts match on Saturday night...' Andy paused for a moment. 'Oh yeah, I almost forgot. Someone tried to shoot me on Friday night.'

Chapter 12

Andy picked up his beer and a glass of rum and coke from the bar, then strolled over to the table where Zephaniah was seated, perusing the *Racing Times*. He put his pint down and grabbed a stool. 'Evening, Zeph,' he said brightly as he placed the rum and coke on the table in front of his friend.

'Don' you sit there, man.' Zephaniah looked up at Andy, his eyes wide.

Andy was puzzled. 'What d'you mean, don't sit there?'

'You ain't sitting anywhere near me, man.'

'Don't be stupid.' As Andy went to sit down, Zephaniah drew back, grabbing his newspaper as he did so.

'No, man. You ain't sitting nowhere near me. You is dangerous.'

Andy hesitated, half-standing, half-seated, 'What d'you mean, dangerous?'

'People die, man. People next to you die. I ain't sitting next to you. I ain't ready to die.'

It then dawned on Andy what his friend was talking about. 'Oh! The shooting. Is that what you're on about?'

'Yeah, man. I sees it in the paper, I know that was you eating fish and chips outside the station with that tramp,

Paddy, like you said you did. You sit over there.' Zephaniah indicated a chair some distance away.

'Okay.' Andy sat down at a table at the other end of the bar.

'Why do they want to kill you, man? What 'ave you done? You a *gangster* or somethin'?' Zephaniah drained his glass in one gulp.

'Zeph, it was just a mistake, an accident. Probably some drunk with a gun just wanted to rid the streets of tramps, I don't know, but it's not contagious.'

'I don' care. You just stay over there. I need another drink. All this stress has made me thirsty. Get me a drink, man, but don' come near me. Leave it over there,' Zephaniah indicated another vacant table, 'and I'll collect it when it's safe.'

Andy ordered a rum and coke and, after perusing the jukebox titles for a few minutes, selected *The Carpenters* and *Leo Sayer* before returning to his seat.

'How are the Mrs Zephaniahs?'

'They is fine, man, but they don' wanna be widows. One widow is bad enough but two, man, that's bad. You jus' keep a safe distance from me.'

'What about me, Zeph? Don't you think I got a bit of a surprise when the man sitting next to me suddenly ends up dead from acute lead poisoning?'

'Yeah, man, mus' 'ave ruined your evenin'.' Zephaniah picked up his *Racing Times* and rose to his feet. 'I'm off to work before I get killed.'

Andy lit his cigarette. 'See you tomorrow.'

'That's if you is still alive.' Zephaniah then headed for the door, skirting round the sides of the room to leave a safe distance between himself and Andy.

***

'Good evening, ma'am. I'm PC Crocker of Clapham Police. Is Mr Norris in?' Lucy stood at the half-opened door of Parkview Cottage watching the uniformed officer rocking gently to and fro on his heels.

'Maybe. What's it all about?' she asked.

'Well, ma'am, I'd like to ask him a few questions. It's about the unexpected and rather sudden death of an itinerant last Friday.'

'Itinerant?' Lucy looked at the police officer questioningly.

'Yes, ma'am. Vagrant or tramp, if you prefer.'

'Oo! You mean the shootin'?'

'Well, not to put too fine a point on it, yes, ma'am.'

'Wasn't that terrible! 'Ave you caught anyone yet?'

'Not exactly, ma'am.'

'Wot d'you mean, "not exactly"?'

'Well, not at all in actuality.'

''Ere, you'd better come in. Andy was scared 'alf out of his wits, I can tell you.' Lucy opened the front door wide to let PC Crocker enter. 'He's in the sitting room at the end on the right.' Then Lucy shouted, 'Andy, it's the cops for you. They 'aven't found the murderer yet.'

As Crocker entered the room, Andy shifted his position from supine to sitting and stubbed out his cigarette.

'Sorry to trouble you this late in the evening, Mr Norris, but we're following up a few leads from the shooting incident on last Friday.'

'Ah, yes. What leads?'

'Well, to be brutally honest – there are none whatsoever, sir. That's why I'm here. The Chief Superintendent thinks it would be helpful to stage a reconstruction.'

'Oh?'

'Yes, repeat the events of the evening in question as near exactly as possible.' Crocker paused for a moment, 'but avoiding the actual killing – obviously.'

'Well, that *would* be difficult as Paddy's gone to that great park bench in the sky.'

'Yes, quite so, sir. Obviously, someone will have to act his part and the Chief Super seems to want me to do that; though, to be frank, I'm not at all sure I'm the best person. But that's not your concern. No, the reason I'm here is that we want *you* to play yourself.' Andy looked puzzled. 'Let me explain, sir. This coming Friday, we want you to retrace your steps and do the very same as you did on the night of the killing. Then, we'll appeal for witnesses.'

Lucy had been listening with increasing concern. 'That sounds dangerous,' she said.

'It's quite safe, ma'am; it's only a reconstruction.'

'You're sure I won't get shot?' Andy looked worried. 'It was a close call last time – and to deliberately do it again seems to me to be asking for trouble.'

'Quite sure. If anything, I'm going to be the one in the firing line, as it were.' Crocker chuckled at his little joke.

'Which do you prefer, plaice or cod?'

'How do you mean, sir?'

'Fish and chips. I used to share them with Paddy. Personally, I prefer plaice.'

'Oh, I see. In the interests of authenticity, I think you should buy exactly the same fish as you did the Friday before last.'

'That'll be plaice then.'

'So can I take it that you're willing to re-enact the evening?' Crocker was looking at Andy but it was Lucy who responded first.

'Andy, are you sure this is sensible? You never know what might 'appen. That gunman is still out there, remember? He may want to kill *you* this time.'

Crocker turned to face Lucy. 'Hardly likely, ma'am. This operation is about appealing for witnesses, jogging their memories, know what I mean? We don't expect the killer to take part in the reconstruction; that's not the idea at all.' PC Crocker frowned and looked up at the ceiling as though attempting to solve a knotty problem; then with a smile, he turned his attention back to Lucy. 'If we were in a position to ask the gunman to take part, we wouldn't need to stage the reconstruction now, would we?'

Andy looked at Lucy and then at Crocker, confusion written all over his face. 'But surely the whole point is...' Andy paused for a moment, trying to comprehend Crocker's logic, then gave up and said, 'Oh, all right then. I'll be doing the same things anyway so I may as well be part of the show.'

'Thank you, sir. I'll be waiting for you on the park bench at nine-thirty.'

'Salt and vinegar?'

'I beg your pardon, sir?'

'Salt and vinegar. What d'you take on your chips?'

'Oh, just salt, please.'

The interview over, Lucy showed PC Crocker to the door and then returned to the sitting room. 'Andy, are you sure this is a good idea?' she asked with obvious concern.

***

'I ain't doin' it, man! You must be mad.'

It was the following night and Andy was trying to convince Zephaniah to take part in the reconstruction. 'All you'll have to do is repeat, as exactly as you can, your actions of Friday night when Paddy the vagrant got shot.'

'But that's the exact same as I do every night. I come in here at six 'o clock, I sit in this chair at this table and pick my losers. Then I go to work at five to nine. Occasionally, a white honkey joins me and buys me a drink but I stopped that when he became a lead magnet.'

'Yeah, Zeph, but you've got to re-enact the scene exactly. That'll mean sitting next to me just as we were last week. There'll be police here asking other customers if they remember anything unusual about the evening. It'll be quite safe.'

'No one's safe next to you, man. I'll be here but I ain't sitting next to you.'

'Oh well, if you won't do your public duty and help me catch a dangerous criminal, then I'll just have to do it on my own.' Andy sighed and lifted his copy of the *Evening Standard*.

***

'Yes Crocker, what do you want?' The Chief Superintendent looked up from the newspaper on the desk in front of him, where he had been reading an article entitled, *Clapham Shooting – Police close in on killer*.

Crocker's usually clean-shaven features were now covered with several days of stubble and he appeared to be dressed as a gardener. 'Well, sir, this may sound strange but something has struck me.'

'Don't talk in riddles, man. What d'you mean something has struck you?'

'Well, I went to see Mr Norris about the reconstruction...' Crocker hesitated.

'Yes! Come along, man. I haven't got all day.'

'...Well, it suddenly struck me.'

'For God's sake, man, *what* struck you?'

'Well, he looks a bit like Vinnie Archer but a younger version.'

'Who does?'

'Mr Norris, sir.'

'How can he? Vinnie Archer is dead.'

Crocker looked puzzled. 'I know, sir.'

'So how can he look like someone who's dead, when he's alive? You're talking rubbish, man.'

'Yes, but Kenny the Giant doesn't know that he's dead.'

'Crocker, you're talking in riddles. Sometimes I wonder about you. How are the bowels?'

'Perfect, sir. Sorry to have troubled you.'

The Chief Super sniffed the air around Crocker. 'Good! Good! I see you're getting into the part of the tramp. Perhaps it would be best if you worked from home until after the reconstruction.'

'Yes, sir.'

Chapter 13

'Here, Lucy, do you realise that you're three million years old?' Andy, who was in his habitual position on the couch, briefly looked up from his newspaper at Lucy who was sitting with a mug of coffee in her hand, gazing uninterestedly at the television.

'Wot you on about?'

'It says here,' Andy looked back at the newspaper and quoted, '*A hominid skeleton has been discovered in Ethiopia and is thought to be three million years old*. And guess what? They've called it Lucy, after you.'

Lucy just grimaced and continued to gaze unseeingly at the screen.

'Are you still upset about Twatface?'

'Well, a bit, I suppose.'

'Do you see much of him at work?'

'That's the problem. I'm stuck at my desk, typing an' that, and he has to pass me every time he goes in or out of his office.'

'Has he said anything – you know – about the weekend?'

'Yeah, he waited for a quiet moment and came over to see me today. Said he wanted to apologise.'

'And?'

'He said he was feverish after bein' out in the rain and didn't know what he was doing. Something about alcohol and some tablets he'd taken affecting him in a strange way.'

'Oh, yeah.'

'He said he couldn't remember anything about snogging Amanda and only came to when I poured the jug of iced water over him.'

'So, are you going to forgive him?'

'Well, the problem is this, Andy. I've never been out with anyone like him before. And let's face it; 'e's a bit of a catch for a girl like me. D'you know what I mean? With 'im, it might be possible for me to break out from being a secretary: a working-class girl from Wapping. A chance to better meself.'

'What's wrong with being a working-class girl from Wapping? You should be proud of it. Are you sure you don't like him for what he represents – an upper-class twit?'

'You don't understand, Andy. I don't want to just drift along, get married, get pregnant, get bored. I want to *do* something with my life. I'm not like you, Andy – I've got ambitions.'

A trifle hurt by this observation, Andy retorted, 'I've got ambitions too.'

'Name one?'

'I want to do a 170-checkout before I'm thirty.'

'You see, Andy, that's your problem. Everything's a joke to you. You can't take anything seriously. I've got *real* ambitions.'

'Such as?'

Lucy took a sip from her mug. 'Oh, I don't know. But I'm sure there's more to life than lying on the couch drinking beer and smoking.'

Andy looked at his can of beer and stubbed out his cigarette. 'So are you seeing him again?'

'He asked me out. Said he wanted to make it up to me.'

'And?'

'I said I'd think about it.' Lucy finished the last of her coffee. 'I'm off to bed now. Goodnight, Andy.'

The following evening, Lucy arrived home with a huge bunch of flowers. She arranged them carefully in a vase that she placed on a mantelshelf in the sitting room. Andy could detect a slight smile on her face. 'So, don't tell me you've accepted another date with Twatface?'

'It's none of your business.' Lucy looked at the flowers from various angles, then added, 'But as it 'appens, yes, I 'ave. And don't call him that. He's just misunderstood, that's all.'

'Is *that* what they call it now?'

***

PC Crocker had really got into the part. He had never done any undercover work before but felt sure that he had a bit of a knack for it and knew that this was a once-in-a-lifetime opportunity to prove himself, to show his worth as a detective. On the afternoon of the day of the reconstruction, he donned his gardening clothes, pulled on a grubby woolly hat and for authenticity, rubbed some rotten sprouts, which he had kept for the purpose, over his outer garments, putting a couple into each of his pockets for good measure. He then filled an old plastic bag with some essentials including a bottle of Robinson's lime juice wrapped in a brown paper bag. Thus disguised, he slipped surreptitiously out of his flat and set off to walk the mile or so to his position on the park bench at Clapham Southside. The weather was fine and he had a spring in his step as he strolled along the side streets heading for the Common. Although not the most observant of individuals, he soon noticed that other pedestrians were avoiding him. Most just kept a wide berth but others actually crossed the road as they saw him approaching. Then a group of teenage boys blocked the pavement in front of him and when he tried to pass, they moved to bar the way. One of them approached and was about to say something abusive when his face wrinkled up. 'Good God! What a stink,' he said as he quickly moved aside.

Crocker was about to reprimand them – as he had other groups of youths so many times in the past – but just in time, he remembered that he was undercover and bit his lip and walked on.

'Filthy tramp,' the youths shouted after him as he once more set off down the road.

As he was nearing the tube station, a sprightly elderly man wearing a beige raincoat and sporting a trilby at a jaunty angle called out: 'You should be ashamed of yourself. I fought for my country and *look* at you.' Crocker desperately wanted to explain that he was really a policeman, a pillar of society, in disguise trying to rid the community of a dangerous criminal. He began to think that this undercover malarkey was not all it was cracked up to be.

As he turned the corner, passing the entrance to Clapham Common tube station and coming in sight of the park bench, he was taken completely by surprise. There, sitting comfortably with his face turned toward the evening sun, was a tramp. He hesitated, not sure what to do, and went to glance at his watch before realising that he was not wearing one but he knew that he was early for his rendezvous. Crocker then did what many of us do in such situations – he jumped to a wholly unjustified and incorrect conclusion. For some bizarre reason, he thought that the Chief Superintendent must have sent another policeman to play the role of the deceased tramp, pending his own arrival.

As he approached the bench, he was gratified to be welcomed with a slight smile from the incumbent tramp. 'It's all right, I'm here now,' Crocker said as he sat down at the other end of the bench.

'Eh?' was all the other man said.

'I said, it's all right; I'll take over now. You can go.'

The vagrant, who was dressed in the same style as Crocker but rather more smartly, looked at him puzzled. 'What d'you mean, I can go? I was here first.'

Crocker did not want to become involved in an unseemly argument with a colleague who was clearly from another constabulary, but wished to complete the operation that he had been given and had trained long and hard for. The reconstruction required one tramp to be on the bench, not two, and Crocker was determined that *he* was going to be that tramp. 'Look,' he said quietly to the incumbent vagrant, 'there's supposed to be only *one* tramp sitting here, so you can go.' Crocker then looked at the other man with admiration. 'By the way,' he said, 'nice disguise. I would never have guessed.'

'Guessed what?'

Crocker glanced around to make sure that they were not being overheard. 'You know, that you're one of *us*.'

'How d'you mean – one of *us*?'

Crocker looked around again then produced his bottle of Robinson's lime juice in its brown paper bag and offered it to the vagrant. 'You know, a boy in blue. Here, have a drink.'

The vagrant, who had previously been struggling with this conversation, was now becoming frankly alarmed. He waved away the brown bag. 'You've been at the juice for too long, mate. You're mad. I'm off.' As the tramp struggled to his feet, his expression changed to one of disgust. 'You stink, mate. It's people like you that give us vagrants a bad name.'

Crocker was confused by his colleague's response but took his place at the end of the bench, took a swig of lime juice and settled back comfortably in the early evening sun to watch the commuters stream out of the station. He did not immediately notice the uniformed police officer approaching him and was startled when he came up to him and said, 'Excuse me, sir, but you'll have to move on. We've a reconstruction this evening and we've commandeered this bench for an undercover officer.' The officer then stepped back quickly as he caught a whiff of Crocker.

'I *am* that policeman,' Crocker replied.

'Of course you are, sir. Now, move along please or I'll have to arrest you for vagrancy.'

It was at that moment that the Chief Super arrived and addressed the policeman, 'Everything all right, constable?'

'I'm just moving this vagrant on, sir, in preparation for the reconstruction.'

The Chief Super, resplendent in a well-ironed uniform and peaked cap, looked at Crocker for a moment before realising who it was. 'Good God, man, is that you, Crocker?'

'Yes, sir.'

The Chief Super turned to the uniformed officer, 'It's all right, constable, he's one of ours.' The uniformed officer withdrew to a safe distance. 'Good disguise, Crocker. Well done. What time is Norris due?'

'Nine thirty, sir.'

'Good, should be here at any time now then.' The Chief Super, his hands clasped behind his back, stood up straight, sniffed the air deeply and then coughed violently. 'I'm sure you'll understand if I move a short distance upwind.' As he wandered away to stand at a discreet distance, a couple of children came up and spat on Crocker who raised his fist angrily at them as they ran off laughing.

Andy Norris, meanwhile, was having a problem getting Zephaniah, who was seated at a table several yards from him, to join in the spirit of the reconstruction.

'Look, Zeph, it's got to be *exactly* the same as two weeks ago.'

'I don' care, man. I ain't sitting near you. It's too risky.'

'Zeph, it's a reconstruction. This whole place is probably crawling with cops.' Andy looked around at the half a dozen or so other customers in the Herald Lounge Bar. He had no idea which ones were the police. However, he vaguely recollected seeing the man with thick glasses wearing a fedora and a long leather coat. *Probably CID,* he thought to himself. *No normal person dresses like that.* Zephaniah made no attempt to move. 'Oh, all right,' Andy said grumpily, 'Stay there then. What music did I put on last week? I can't remember.'

'All I know was that it wasn't Mrs Mills.'

'Must have been the New Seekers then.'

'Anythin' but Mrs Mills, man.'

'Now you're getting the hang of it.'

Zeph looked up, puzzled, 'How d'you mean, man?'

'That's what you said on the night of the shooting.'

'That's 'cos that's what I always say.'

'How many pints did I have last week, Zeph? Can you remember?'

'No idea, man. Too many, that's for sure.'

The pair of them then sat at their respective tables, reading their newspapers and occasionally swapping comments until Zephaniah announced that it was time for him to go to work.

Andy was now in his habitual half-inebriated state but determined to act out his part as accurately as possible. He ordered another pint, lit a cigarette and finished reading his newspaper. At what he thought was the appropriate time, he folded the paper, put it in his pocket and, with a breezy farewell to the barman, headed for the door. It was beginning to rain outside so Andy hurried to Bank Station and descended to the Northern Line platform where the doors of a southbound train were beginning to close. Showing remarkable speed for an obese man with seven pints on board, he reached the train just in time to squeeze between the doors as they closed.

What happened next was probably partly due to the fact that Andy had not been sleeping as well as usual and, that in his somewhat tense state of mind, had consumed three more pints than normal. He fell soundly asleep.

Myopic Mick felt smug. He had been right all along. Vinnie Archer had tried to double-bluff him and there he was, in exactly the same position as he had been the previous week. His minder, however, he noticed was seated a few tables away. *Wise precaution,* Mick thought to himself, *better able to monitor potential threats that way and avoid being in the same line of fire. Clever. Very clever.*

When Andy rose to leave the bar, Mick was ready. He felt the reassuring bulge of his revolver in his leather coat, got up and casually followed him. He was confident that Archer would take the same route home so was happy to keep an eye on him from a distance of about fifty yards. Mick smiled to himself as his quarry turned into Bank Station and then he followed him down the escalators to the Northern Line platform. Then the man he was following did something he did not expect. He began to run and to Mick's amazement, just managed to enter a carriage before the doors closed. Although by now only a few yards behind, Mick was too late and could only watch as the train pulled away with his target on board.

For a moment, he was furious but then remembered that he had predicted everything that Archer had done so far and there was no reason to believe that he would do anything different now. 'A man of habit is our Vinnie,' Mick said quietly to himself as he waited impatiently for the next southbound train. Fifteen minutes later, he alighted at Clapham Common Station where he briefly glanced around the platform but was not surprised when there was no sign of his target.

Mick ran up the escalator and walked out on to the street outside the station where, after a brief look around, he crossed the road and headed for the North Sea Fish Bar. To his surprise, Archer was not there either. He was now concerned that Archer had deliberately given him the slip. He rushed back across the road and headed for the park bench and the site of the previous week's shooting.

As he approached, he was surprised to see a tramp sitting there. He could not recollect what the tramp he had shot looked like as he had been concentrating on Archer at the time, but this one looked similar. *But then,* he thought to himself, *they all look much the same. There's no reason why another tramp shouldn't have taken up residence on the same seat – this is probably a prime site for vagrants.* Then, after just a moment's hesitation, Mick walked directly up to the man seated on the bench. 'Excuse me,' he said, 'has there been a man sitting here eating fish and chips in the last few minutes?'

'No,' replied the tramp. 'We're waiting for him as well.'

Mick was confused. 'What do you mean, "we're waiting for him as well"?'

'He was due here about ten minutes ago and we're still waiting. We're not sure what's happened to him.'

Mick was wondering what on earth the tramp meant when he noticed two uniformed police officers twenty yards away heading in his direction so he turned to make his getaway as casually as he could. As he made his way to Kenny's safe house, he was trying to work out how Vinnie could have vanished into thin air.

As Crocker and Mick were discussing the whereabouts of Archer, his doppelgänger, Andy, was to be found sound asleep snoring loudly as the tube train rattled ever further south. It was only when the train came to a standstill at Morden did Andy awake and realise what had happened. He glanced at his watch and, on discovering that there was just enough time to make it back before the chip shop closed, hurried across the platform to board the waiting northbound train on the opposite side.

Chapter 14

'Make us a coffee.' Andy shouted in the general direction of the kitchen, without taking his eyes off the newspaper he was reading.

'Make it yourself,' yelled Lucy in response.

'Oh go on, *please*.'

'All right, but you're a lazy bastard, Andy Norris.'

'I know I am.'

It was the day after the crime reconstruction and Andy was perusing the morning papers from his usual position on the couch. 'Looks like they'll have to call an election unless the miners go back to work,' he said as his housemate entered the sitting room.

Lucy handed him a mug of coffee and took a seat. ''Ow did the reconstruction go?'

'Well, to be honest, I rather messed it up.'

'Typical! Wot 'appened?'

'I fell asleep on the tube and woke up at Morden. By the time I got back, it was all over. Everyone had gone home except for a smelly old tramp sitting on the bench where Paddy used to sit.'

'That policeman was supposed to be the tramp, wasn't he? You know, him wot came around.'

'I know, it *was* him but his disguise was so good that I didn't realise to start with. Anyway, I apologised for being late and he said everyone had left apart from him. He said he'd been worried about me and had decided to wait to see if I came back safely.'

'Wot did he mean by *if* you came back safely?'

'Well, that's the thing, Lucy. I'm beginning to think that the coppers think I might be the next target. Anyway, I'm going to the police station later on this afternoon. They want to talk to me about something.'

'You've done all you can, Andy, so why don't you just forget about it now?'

'You're probably right but I'll go along and see what it's all about. I hope Crocker's had a bath by then. He smelled really dreadful.'

''Ave you got a darts match tonight?'

'Yeah. The Dog and Duck – home match. We'll be thrashed as usual. Do you want to come along?'

'No thanks, Andy. Nigel's coming round.'

'Oh. D'you want me to stay out late?'

'Don't be so filthy. Nigel's not like that.'

'Like what?'

'You know.'

'Is he a poof as well as a twat?'

'Shut up, Andy.'

Andy just shook his head. 'I don't know what you see in that man.' Andy thought for a moment. 'Well, apart from his good looks.'

Lucy gazed into the middle distance. 'And his charm.'

'His politeness?'

'Yeah. Then there's 'is car.'

'And he's rich.'

'Intelligent.'

Andy was silent for a moment, thoughtful. 'Yes, maybe; but apart from all that, he's a twat. What are you doing tonight?'

'He's going to take me out for a pub supper.'

Andy put his paper down on the floor beside him, a hint of interest now registering on his face. 'That's great, Lucy. Bring him along to the Nellie. You can watch the darts and have a meal there. They do jellied eels, hot pies and several different flavours of crisps.'

'I think he's got something else in mind.'

'I'll bet he has.'

'Stop being dirty. I think he's got something a bit posher than jellied eels in mind.'

'Okay, Lucy. Have a good evening. I'd better get off to the police station.

**

'You remember PC Crocker, Mr Norris?' The Chief Superintendent had ushered Andy into his office, which smelt strangely of rotting vegetation. Crocker, who was seated near the chief's desk, nodded his recognition. His face was a patchwork of red and pink where he had struggled to shave off his beard that morning with a less-than-sharp razor.

'Yes, of course.' Andy took the seat offered to him, facing the Chief Superintendent who had settled into his swivel chair behind his desk. 'Sorry about last night. I got a bit carried away in the pub and what with all the stress of the last week, I haven't been sleeping too well.'

'Never mind, Norris. Very important – sleep. Bowels okay?'

'Yes, thanks. You?'

'Every day, just like clockwork. Don't need a timepiece with bowels like mine.' The Chief Super swivelled violently in his chair to face Andy. 'Now, we're not here to discuss my bowels, important though they are. Are we, Crocker?' The Chief swivelled back to face his subordinate.

'No, sir.'

'We're here to discuss the shooting just a week and one day ago. It's still a mystery but Crocker here has done some thinking and come up with an interesting idea, haven't you, Crocker?'

'Yes, sir.'

'Crocker's idea is that it wasn't the tramp that was the target, Mr Norris, but *you*.' The Chief Super had swivelled again and was now beginning to feel a trifle dizzy.

Andy's eyes widened. 'That's crazy. Why on earth would anyone want to shoot me?'

'Excellent question, Norris. We have been wrestling with that little conundrum for some time, haven't we, Crocker?'

'We have, sir.'

'And we've come up with an answer, haven't we?'

'Yes, sir.'

'And the answer, Crocker, is?'

Crocker leant forward. 'It appears—'

The Chief Super interrupted, 'Well, I'll tell you. It's because you *look* like a criminal.'

This was too much for Andy. He knew he was overweight, badly dressed and drank too much but he had never been told that he looked like a criminal.

'That's outrageous. I do *not* look like a criminal,' Andy said defensively.

'I don't mean you look like just *any* old criminal. You look like one in particular.'

'Oh?'

'Yes. Crocker has spotted a likeness, haven't you, Crocker?'

'Yes, sir.'

'And that likeness is with whom, Crocker?' The Chief did not wait for an answer. 'Well, I'll tell you. One Vinnie Archer, sometimes known as *The Bowman*.' The Chief then sat back in his chair to let this bombshell sink in.

Andy's normally vacuous face now took on an expression of puzzlement over which lay a fine veneer of vagueness. He knew the name was familiar but he could not quite place it. Then suddenly he remembered reading about the trial of Kenny Craft and how Vinnie Archer had turned Queen's evidence to avoid prosecution. 'I remember now,' he said excitedly. 'He was the one who shopped his mate who then escaped during a power cut.'

'Exactly, Mr Norris. And our escaped criminal, one Kenny the Giant Craft, is a trifle upset about the aforementioned events and is looking for retribution.'

'Why choose me? Surely I don't look that much like him? Why not go after the real Vinnie?'

'Ah, for one very good reason.'

'And what is that one very good reason?' asked Andy who was becoming increasingly perplexed.

'Because he's dead, isn't he, Crocker?'

'Yes, sir.'

'In that case, why is he trying to kill someone who's already dead?'

'Because we haven't told him that he's dead. That's why. We have deliberately kept his death a secret so that Craft will come out of hiding to kill him – or rather *you*.'

'Then for heaven's sake, will someone please tell him he's dead so that he'll stop trying to shoot me?'

'But then we won't catch our escaped prisoner now, will we, Mr Norris? The situation, as I see it, is quite simple. Isn't it, Crocker?'

'Probably, sir.'

'I'm going to be blunt, Norris. It's clear to me that, like it or not, sometime soon you're going to get horribly murdered as Craft thinks you're Vinnie Archer. You may as well join forces with us and become an official decoy. That way, you'll get killed at a time and place of our choosing and we can arrest Craft as soon as he's performed the act. Sounds good, doesn't it?'

'Not particularly,' said Andy who did not share the Chief Superintendent's enthusiasm for the plan.

'But you've got nothing to lose. You're going to get shot anyway so you may as well die usefully.'

Crocker coughed to attract the attention of his superior. 'Excuse me, sir.'

'Yes, Crocker.'

'Well, sir, it has just occurred to me that we might be able to catch our man without Mr Norris here having to die in the process.'

Andy and the Chief Super looked at PC Crocker enquiringly. 'We could arrange a sting operation. I've seen it done on television, sir. We let the underworld know where Archer (that is, Mr Norris here) will be at a certain time and arrange for undercover officers to be there and catch Kenny Craft *before* he can kill him horribly.'

'That sounds like a better plan to me,' said Andy with an enthusiasm he had not felt since the beginning of the interview.

The Chief sat back in his swivel chair with his head tilted upwards, his eyes closed and his fingertips together. After a moment, he opened his eyes, swung violently round to face Andy and said, 'I know what we'll do. We'll set Craft up. We'll make him think that Vinnie Archer will be in a certain place at a certain time and send you along. But we'll flood the place with plain-clothes officers and if Craft takes the bait, we'll catch him; hopefully, before he gets a chance to kill you. It's brilliant! Nothing can possibly go wrong.' The senior officer sat back in his chair with an expression of satisfaction on his face. 'How about it, Norris?'

'It still sounds a bit risky to me.'

'Of course, it is. A hundred and one things could go wrong but the alternative is that you'll get shot at a time and place not of your own choosing and with no hope of rescue by my chaps. This, at least, you've got a sporting chance of not getting yourself killed and you'll be helping us catch a dangerous criminal to boot.'

***

'So, Mick, what have you got to tell me, eh? Say something I want to hear; something that's music to my ears.' Kenny Craft dropped his gaze from the picture of the Virgin Mary and turned to face his hitman who had just arrived back at the safe house. 'Tell me that Vinnie Archer is dead.' His voice dropped to a menacing whisper. 'That's what I want to hear. Anything else isn't good enough, Mick. D'you understand?'

'I brought your favourite, Kenny. It's sausage and chips tonight, with brown sauce.'

'Mick, I don't care what's on the menu tonight. I want to know if the Bowman is dead. That's all I want to hear. Get it? *Is Vinnie dead*?'

Mick hesitated for a moment while he put his shopping bag down. 'Well, to be honest, Kenny, not quite.'

'What d'you mean, *not quite*?'

'Well, he obviously knew that he was being followed and made a dash for it and I lost him on the tube.'

'That's not very good, is it, Mick? That's not even *nearly* dead.'

'The interesting thing though, Kenny, is that there was a tramp sitting on the bench the same as last week. He could be the same one for all I know. Anyway, I asked him if Vinnie had been there and he said something very strange.'

'What did he say, Mick?'

'Well, he said that they were waiting for him as well.'

'*They*?'

'Yes, *they,* as though there were other tramps waiting.'

'Interesting.' Kenny gazed at the Virgin Mary, concentration written all over his face. 'This is all becoming very interesting. Maybe the tramp wasn't killed – maybe that's the story the cops have put out – what they want us to think. Maybe, just maybe, there's a whole army of tramps out there acting as Vinnie's undercover eyes and ears. Know what I mean?' Kenny looked at the assassin meaningfully. 'Maybe you missed both of them last week. Your eyesight's not what it used to be, is it, Mick?'

Mick chose not to answer the query but continued his report. 'That's not all, Kenny; I saw two policemen hovering nearby, questioning passers-by.'

'How d'you know they were real policemen, Mick? They could be tramps disguised as police officers.' Kenny was thoughtful. 'You know what, Mick? This whole thing stinks. It smells of Crocker. This has got Crocker written all over it.' Kenny tapped the side of his nose, 'I can smell Crocker a mile away. He's a clever bastard.'

'Well, come to think of it, there was a nasty smell around the park bench, that's for sure.'

'Trust me, Mick. Crocker's behind this. He's clever – very clever.'

'What'll we do now, Kenny?'

'I need to do some 'ard thinking. When you're up against a man like Crocker, you need to think, then think

131

again; and when you think you've thought enough, you think once more.'

Mick frowned. 'I beg your pardon?'

'I need to get under Crocker's skin, anticipate his every move. A bit like you and Vinnie, only better.'

'Shall I do some thinkin' as well?'

'No, that's not your forte, Mick. Put the sausages on. I'm hungry.'

Chapter 15

'But, Lucy dear, he's a complete fraud.'

'Wot d'you mean, a fraud?'

'He not all he says he is.'

'How d'you mean, Lucinda?'

Lucy had travelled across the Albert Bridge to Lucinda's flat in Chelsea in response to an invitation to tea.

'Well, I only know what Rodney says and that's hardly reliable, I would agree, but Nigel's background seems a bit – well, shady. He has lots of airs and graces but Rodney says that he only went to Marlborough for one term and was expelled for stealing. Rodney's not sure what happened then as he wasn't heard of for about ten years. The next thing Rodney knows is that he pitches up at that ghastly law firm as though he's Rodney's best friend. Now Rodney, as you know, is totally untrustworthy but he's hardly likely to make up a story like that.

'He's still a lawyer though. That's all right, isn't it?'

'Well, I think that you'll find he's what's called a legal assistant.'

'I wondered why he wasn't listed on the notepaper. 'Ow did he get invited to that party then?'

'I've absolutely no idea, but Rupert doesn't know him from Adam. I suspect he used Rodney's name to inveigle an invitation from Rupert's secretary. He's a social climber, Lucy, the very worst type of conman.'

Lucy was silent for a while. 'But he's got a posh name.'

'Not really. Bernard, I gather, is his middle name, that's all. There are no Bernard-Fieldings that I'm aware of. But Lucy, I didn't invite you over to discuss your boyfriend. For all I know, he might be an absolute charmer and the right man for you but I thought you should be aware that all may not be as it seems.' Lucinda took a sip of tea and then replaced her porcelain cup on its saucer. 'No, apart from wanting to meet up with you again after your sterling performance at the shooting party, I wanted to ask a favour of you.'

'A favour? Of course. What is it?'

'Well, Rupert was wondering if we might come over and see you some time.'

Lucy's eyes widened. 'But I can't put on a party like that. I'm in rented accommodation. I share with Andy. I couldn't possibly...'

'Lucy, dear, don't panic. We don't want you to have a party in your house. What Rupert would like is if you could show him a slice of London life, in the raw as it were. Rupert took a real shine to you at his party and it made him realise how sheltered his life has been. If I didn't know that he loves me to distraction, I might even be ever so slightly jealous. Anyway, Rupert is fed up with the sycophants and hangers-on that seem to accompany him everywhere and wondered if you might be able to show him a side of London that he doesn't know: you know, jellied eels and that sort of thing. You're a Londoner and we thought you might be able to help.'

'Oooh, I dunno about that. I'd be a bit worried taking you around Wapping.'

'Well, what about Clarm? There must be some excellent pubs there.'

'Clarm?' said Lucy, puzzled.

'Yes, Clarm. Where you live. You *do* live there, don't you?' Lucinda looked at Lucy questioningly for a moment before her expression changed to one of understanding. 'Oh, you probably call it Clapham.'

'Yeah, most people do. Look, I'll think about it and give you a ring tomorrow.'

'Thank you, Lucy. I do so want to help Rupert in his endeavour as I really think he's about to throw in the towel and ask me to marry him.'

***

'Come in, Crocker.'

'You asked to see me, sir.'

The Chief Super put down his copy of *Keep Regular, Keep Fit*, and swivelled to face the police constable. 'Yes, so I did. I thought we should discuss our sting operation.' He was pensive for some time. 'You know, Crocker, if we put Kenny back behind bars where he belongs, there could be promotion in it for us both.'

'That would be good, sir.'

'Yes. Maybe Chief Constable for me and no more lost property and stray dogs for you. Talking of which, any leads on the stolen bike?'

'Well, there has been some movement, sir.'

'Movement. I like that, Crocker.'

'There was a possible sighting on the Common last week but sadly the trail has now gone cold.'

'Never mind. Bigger fish now, Crocker.' The Super sniffed the air. 'What's that smell?'

'What smell, sir?'

'Smells like vegetables.'

'Oh, that'll be the sprouts, sir.'

'Sprouts?'

'Yes, sir, I've found it very difficult to eradicate the smell.'

The Chief Super's brow creased with confusion. 'Ah, yes – whatever. I've been thinking. In my opinion, a pub would be a good place to lure our friend Kenny into the open. We put it about that Vinnie will be in such and such a pub on such and such an evening, then plant our friend Mr Norris there and wait for the fireworks to begin. Pretty good plan, don't you think?'

'Brilliant, sir. Where were you thinking of?'

'That's where I need your help. Clapham was Kenny's patch so somewhere local would seem appropriate. Any ideas?'

Crocker was thoughtful. 'We mustn't place the public in danger so we'd need the landlord on our side.'

'Absolutely, but some collateral damage may be unavoidable.'

'I think the Lord Nelson would be a good bet. We've worked with the landlord before on the case of the missing pint glasses, do you remember?'

'Yes, nasty business that. Got a conviction, as I recall.'

'Not as such.'

'But we found the glasses?'

'True. However, all but one was broken in the chase.'

'Well, never mind. Bigger fish, Crocker, bigger fish! Now, you must speak to the manager of The Nelson and with Norris to set a date. Remember, our injunction runs out at the end of next week and then the press will have a heyday. Once Kenny knows that Archer is dead, he'll go underground for good. That is...' the Chief Super looked at Crocker knowingly, '...until he comes after you!'

***

'So, Mr Norris. What would be a good day for you?' PC Crocker was seated in the armchair at Parkview where he had outlined operation 'Catch Kenny' to Andy and Lucy.

Lucy's face registered concern. 'Are you sure this is a good idea, Andy? It sounds like it might be dangerous.'

For once, Andy was sitting rather than lying on the settee. 'I'm no happier about it than you are, Lucy. But according to the boys in blue here, I have little choice. Either the assassin kills me at some random time and in an unforeseen place or I get shot at a venue and time of our choosing with half a chance that Crocker here and his men might, just might, catch the Giant before he kills me. Is that a fair summary?' Andy looked at Crocker.

'Very nicely put, if I might say so, sir.'

'And let me get this straight. You and your men will be at the pub in disguise.'

'Yes, sir. We'll be dressed as your average South London boozer having a jolly good night out.'

'You're not going to dress up as a tramp again, are you?'

'No, sir.'

'Nothing personal but there was an unpleasant smell.'

'Yes, I know, sir. You were not alone in noticing that. I think I overdid the sprouts.'

Lucy wrinkled her nose. 'Ugh!'

'The devil's vegetable,' added Andy. 'Banned by the Royal Navy in some ships of the line because of their unpleasant effect on the bowels.'

'The Chief Super is very keen on that.'

'Keen on what? Flatulence?'

'No, sir. Regularity.' Crocker paused for a moment, trying to remember why they had got on to the subject of the lower gastrointestinal tract. 'Now, where were we? Ah yes. I'm pleased to say that on this occasion, we'll be dressed as locals and commuters having a quiet beer while enjoying the company of our fellow human beings.'

'Where have you in mind for this undercover operation?'

'We, that is, the Chief Super and I, thought that the Lord Nelson on the other side of the Common would be the best place. It's quiet, set back from the main road and we've worked with the landlord on another case in the past.'

'I thought that you wanted some place where people would have a quiet beer while enjoying the company of their fellow human beings. Hardly likely there, mate.'

'On this occasion, we would close it to the public and fill it with our own men. The kind of officers who *do* like a quiet beer with their fellow human beings.'

'That'll be a first for the Lord Nellie. We beat them quite easily last time.'

'Beat them?'

'Darts.'

'Oh!'

'Will you be there?' asked Andy.

'Yes, but you probably won't recognise me as I'll be undercover and I'm beginning to think I have a natural bent for disguises. You see, Kenny knows me from a previous investigation – a particularly nasty bicycle theft. The details are classified but I was instrumental in his arrest and imprisonment.'

'For a stolen bicycle. That seems a bit harsh,' Andy's voice registered surprise.

'No. It was just that I happened to be questioning him and one of his fellow ne'er-do-wells about the aforementioned bicycle when they owned up to other, even more heinous crimes.'

'Cor. That's amazing.' Lucy looked at Crocker, her eyes wide with admiration.

'All in a day's work, ma'am.' PC Crocker turned back to face Andy. 'We think Thursday would be best, Mr Norris. That way, the landlord won't lose too many customers. You see, we'll have to compensate him for lost business so from the fiscal point of view, the sooner you get killed the better; although,' added Crocker hastily, 'obviously we hope that won't happen.'

'Thursday it is then.'

'Andy, I know you've got other things on your mind at present, wot with this sting operation an' everythin', but I need your 'elp.'

Crocker had just left and Andy and Lucy were chatting. 'My help! That's novel. In what way?'

'You know that woman Lucinda wot I met at the shooting party? Well, she wants to come down here with her friend Rupert. He's the one who owns the country house. They want to go out for a drink, you know, get a feel for city life, Lord knows why. Anyway, I said I'd try and 'elp.'

'Happy to help, Lucy. Is that Twatface Nigel coming along?'

'Yeah, I think I'll ask him along.' Lucy smiled to herself.

'Are you up to something, Lucy?'

'Wot? Me?' Her face was the epitome of innocence, 'Nevva.' Then she began to giggle.

'Well, Lucy, it had better be tomorrow evening as after that, it might be too late. I think we should go the Bell and throw some darts.'

'That's great. Thanks, Andy. And you will behave, won't you?'

'What d'you mean, behave?'

'Well, you know – sometimes after you've had a few beers, you get a bit argumentative and call people things.'

'Like what?'

'Twats.'

'That's an absolute calumny.' Lucy looked at Andy. 'Oh, all right then, I'll behave.'

Chapter 16

'Hey, man, you must be mad.'

'It's not my idea, Zeph.'

'You must have some sort of death wish, man. Volunteering to get killed an' all.'

Andy looked across at Zephaniah who was seated several yards away on the opposite side of the Herald Lounge Bar. 'I haven't volunteered to get killed, Zeph; I'm just going to be acting as a kind of decoy. Anyway, I'm not supposed to talk about it as it's classified.'

'What you mean classified, man? Classified as what – stupid?'

'No, it's a top-secret operation, you know – all hush hush.'

'The only operation you need, man, is a brain transplant.' Zephaniah looked up from his *Racing Times*. 'Anyway, if it's all so secret, why are you telling me then?'

'Well, I thought that maybe, just maybe, if I wasn't here next week, you might wonder what had happened to me.'

'You'd better leave some money behind the bar then, man, just in case you is killed and can't buy your round.' Zephaniah peered at his newspaper. 'What d'you think, Heaven's Mercy or Jack the Lad?'

'What are you talking about?'

'Gee-gees, man. Heaven's Mercy at 9 to 1 or Jack the Lad at 7 to 2 favourite?'

'No idea, Zeph. What's the going like?'

'Soft – like your brain, man.'

'I'd go for Jack the Lad if I was you.'

'Okay, man. But if I lose, you owe me.'

'And if you win?'

'You *don't* owe me. Now, are you buyin' me a drink or what?'

Andy rose from his seat, placed his *Evening News* on the table in front of him and headed for the jukebox. 'Mrs Mills all right?'

'I told you, man, never – *never* – put on Mrs Mills. If you put Mrs Mills on, I'll kill you myself. And leave my drink over there, man. I don't want you comin' anywhere near me.'

Andy wandered over to the bar, ordered a rum and coke and a pint of lager, then returned to his seat and began to read his newspaper. 'By the way, Zeph, I won't be in tomorrow so you'll have to buy your own drinks.'

'Why's that, man? Is you practising getting' yourself killed?'

'No. I'm taking some toffs to a pub in Clapham.'

'Do those toffs know they is riskin' their lives just by bein' near you? Did you tell them that the last person to sit next to you, that tramp, was shot to pieces and is now an ex-tramp?'

'I didn't get him killed. He just happened to be sitting on the same park bench, that's all.'

Zephaniah looked up from his paper. 'Okay, man. Pretend I'm a toff. Ask me to come to Clapham with you.'

'What?'

'I said – ask me to come to Clapham with you.'

Andy put down his paper and looked at his friend in amazement. 'What d'you mean?'

'Just say it, man.'

Andy shook his head and sighed. 'Oh, all right. Come to Clapham with me tomorrow.'

Zephaniah burst into peals of laughter. 'No thanks, man. I'm a toff and everythin' there's *too* common.'

'Eh?'

'Too common, man. Geddit? Clapham Common.' Still chuckling loudly, Zeph peered once more at his copy of the *Racing Times*.

***

'But Nigel, Rupert will be there.' Andy could hear the sound of a voice on the other end of the line but could not make out what Nigel was saying to Lucy.

'Just a few beers, maybe a game of darts, that sort of thing.' Lucy looked up from the telephone receiver and smiled at Andy.

'I'm not sure. Andy said somewhere local.'

'Good. Come round about six o'clock.'

'Bye.'

Lucy put the phone back in its cradle. 'For some reason, he didn't seem too keen to come along tomorrow.'

'What are you playing at, Lucy?'

'I just want to find out what kind of bloke Nigel really is.'

'Why didn't he want to come along?'

'I'm not sure, Andy, but when I mentioned that Rupert was coming, he changed his mind.'

'Is Rupert the posh toff? The thirteenth twatface or something?'

'Andy, you stop that. You promised not to be rude about my friends.'

'I'll try, Lucy, I promise, but I hope they don't push me too far. I have my own street cred to think about as well, you know.'

***

'But it could be a trap, Kenny.'

'Mick, I'm coming with you. Firstly, I can't trust you to shoot the right person; the way things are going, you might have to kill half of London before you get the right man. And secondly, I can't stay cooped up here any longer. I need to get out or I'll go mad.' Kenny the Giant Craft who had been pacing around the room, stopped and gazed out of the window of the safe house. 'How reliable is the information?'

'It's as good as it gets, for sure. I heard the same story from two reliable sources. There can be no doubt that Vinnie's got a deal on and he's set up a meeting in the Nellie on Thursday.' Mick looked at the picture of the Virgin Mary. 'Nice-looking girl,' he whispered quietly to himself.

Kenny resumed his pacing around the room like a caged tiger. 'For Christ's sake, concentrate, Mick.'

'That's blasphemy, Kenny. You shouldn't say things like that.'

Kenny ignored the comment. 'It's Crocker I worry about. It's possible he's behind this.'

'I could go in first, Kenny. He doesn't know me. I could check out if Vinnie's there with his cronies or if the place is full of cops, and then do the business.'

'I'm not letting you do the business until I've seen him for myself. D'you understand?'

'Don't you trust me, Kenny?'

'No, Mick. Frankly, I don't.'

'Tell you what, Kenny. Why don't I go and recce the place tomorrow? Nose about a bit. See what's kicking off?'

'Okay, but leave your shooter behind. I don't want you killing anyone on the off chance that it might be Vinnie. Now, what's for supper?'

***

'Now, men, this will be your final briefing before operation *Catch Kenny*.' The Chief Superintendent was standing in front of a group of ten of his best officers who were seated in the operations room of Clapham Police Station. The Chief was the only one in the room in uniform; the others were wearing an extraordinary variety of costumes. Several were dressed in unseasonably colourful, short-sleeved shirts and shorts; others sported business suits; while at least two looked as though they were extras in a Western. Crocker had been concerned that he would be recognised by Kenny Craft so he had gone the extra mile and come dressed as a scoutmaster. He wore baggy knee-length khaki shorts, a shirt of a similar colour on which he had sewn an impressive array of badges, while perched on his head was the wide-brimmed hat made famous by Lord Baden-Powell. He had particularly favoured this disguise as the hat shielded his face.

The Chief Super looked at his men and nodded slowly. 'Excellent disguises, men. Now, Crocker here is leading this operation as he knows the key players and can recognise them. You must remember that you are a normal bunch of locals going for a pint or two on the way home from work. You are quintessential London boozers. Got that?' A murmur of acquiescence rumbled from the chief's audience. 'Now, men, Kenny is dangerous. Never underestimate him. He has already killed one man and one more victim will mean nothing to him. He's on the run and is vicious when cornered. We are gambling that he will risk coming into the open to kill Vinnie Archer.'

One of the film extras raised his hand. 'But Vinnie Archer is dead, sir.'

'*I* know that and *you* know that, but luckily Kenny Craft doesn't.' The Chief Super looked around the room before continuing. 'And how do we know? Well, I'll tell you: because he has attempted to kill him once already.'

The film extra was now becoming confused. 'Sorry, sir, but how can he attempt to kill someone who's already dead?'

'Because he mistook someone else for him. That's how. And we have identified that man and persuaded him to be a decoy. He has agreed to be in the Lord Nelson on Thursday night on the understanding that everyone else in the bar will be police officers in disguise and will try to protect him from getting shot.' The Chief looked at his officers to make sure that they were keeping up with him. 'Clear so far?' Satisfied by some grunts and nods from those around the room, he continued, 'Now, here is a picture of Craft taken at the time of his trial. You will see that he's a slim, short man.'

The film extra raised his hand again. 'Why's he called *the Giant* then?'

'Satire, constable, satire.'

'Oh.' The would-be cowboy turned to his neighbour who appeared to be dressed as a Red Indian and whispered, 'What's that?'

The Chief ignored him and continued, 'He will be armed and your job is to identify and disarm him, preferably before he's had a chance to kill our decoy, or anyone else for that matter. Now, can anyone here play darts?'

'I can, sir,' said one of the besuited businessmen.

'Good! You can pretend to be having a game of darts and the rest of you are just having a good old time in the pub. I want lots of laughter, joshing and that sort of thing. Do I make myself clear?'

The dart-throwing businessman stood up. 'Are we allowed to drink, sir? You know, being on duty an' all?'

'On this occasion, yes. Clearly, it would look strange if all the customers in the bar were sipping small glasses of grapefruit juice. But no drunkenness! You'll need to keep your wits about you to catch Kenny, believe me. He's a clever bastard. Now, any other questions?'

'Can we claim for the drinks on expenses?'

'For heaven's sake, I suppose so but only the first one – and no doubles or fancy expensive cocktails. Is that clear?'

Crocker now raised his arm. 'What happens if Craft doesn't show, sir?'

'Good question.' The Chief Superintendent squinted at the scoutmaster. 'Is that you, Crocker?'

'Yes, sir.'

'Excellent; I nearly didn't recognise you myself. No sprouts this time, I hope?'

'No, sir.'

'Good. Where was I? Oh yes, if he hasn't arrived by 10 pm, we'll abort the operation.' The Chief Super then paused and when no more questions were forthcoming, drew the meeting to a conclusion. 'All right. That's all for now. I want you in the bar having a good old time at 6 pm tomorrow. Got that?'

'Yes, sir,' rumbled the reply from around the room.

Chapter 17

'Lucy dear, how wonderful to see you.' Lucinda stepped into Parkview and hugged her friend in that no-touch, distant fashion intended not to disturb make up or crease clothing. 'It's so kind of you and your friend to take us out tonight.' She turned to the man standing behind her who was dressed from head to toe in tweed. 'You remember Rupert, I'm sure?'

''Ow can I forget when I did the Gay Gordons with 'im?'

Rupert smiled a toothy, slightly unbalanced smile. 'How nice to meet you again,' he said as Lucy took his proffered hand and curtseyed.

'Come in. Nigel and Andy are waiting indoors.'

Once in the sitting room, Lucy made the introductions. 'Lucinda, you know Nigel, and this is my housemate, Andy.'

'Nigel, I do hope you've brought a spare pair of trousers with you tonight?' Lucinda smiled sweetly as though she had said nothing in any way indiscreet and they shook hands. Then turning to Andy, she said, 'Andrew, how nice to meet you at last. I've heard so much about you. It's good of you to take us out. Let me introduce you to Rupert.'

Rupert gave Andy a warm disarming smile. 'Andy, it's most kind of you to show us the sights.'

Andy emptied his can of beer. 'To be honest, Rupert, there's not much around here to show you but I'm always more than happy to go for a beer.'

'Luce, ol' thing, can I leave the Midget here?'

Lucinda looked at Lucy and rolled her eyes. 'Yes, Nigel, that'll be fine. We're not going far and we'll walk.'

Moments later, the five of them strolled along Clapham Common Southside, chatting and enjoying the fresh, early-spring evening. After about twenty minutes, they reached The Bell, a large and popular pub in the middle of the Common. There, they drank beer and gins and tonics, played darts, ate jellied eels and pies along with several different flavours of crisps. Andy was in in his element, while Lucinda, Rupert and Lucy were becoming quietly and pleasantly inebriated. Only Nigel seemed ill at ease.

After some two hours, Andy looked at his watch. 'Mickey Mouse says it's half past eight so I suggest we move on to another pub.' Andy drained his pint mug and slammed it down on to the table rather more emphatically than he had intended.

'I'm up for that.' Rupert lifted his half-full mug and proceeded to pour the contents down the front of his tweed waistcoat.

Lucinda rather more elegantly finished her gin and tonic and announced, 'Yes, Andrew, I agree. We should sample the delights of another of Clarm's hostelries.'

'Where are you thinking of, Andy, ol' thing?' Nigel discretely placed his unfinished beer on a neighbouring table as they rose to leave.

'The Nell Gwyn.'

'The Nell Gwyn?' Nigel raised his eyebrows. 'Is that wise?'

'Of course it's wise.'

'It's a bit rough.'

'How do you know? Have you been there recently?' asked Andy, surprised.

'No! No. Not personally, but I've heard it's a bit rough.'

'Rubbish. Rupert here wants a slice of South London life. Where better to get it than the Nellie? If there's a fight going on, so much the better.'

They meandered somewhat unsteadily along the northside of the Common to a small side street called Rookery Road, down which they walked the short distance to a pub, where the swinging sign outside depicting a busty woman declared it to be the Nell Gwyn. This was a traditional Victorian corner pub. With its linoleum floors, hand pumps and a limited supply of drinks other than whisky and beer, it had not changed in over fifty years. Heavily stained tables were placed around the periphery of the room while rickety wooden chairs were scattered about randomly. When the little group entered the bar, a pall of smoke greeted them and a silence, almost palpable, descended on the room as the occupants ceased their chatter and took a moment to assess the new arrivals. Two men standing near the dartboard, darts in hand, paused in their game to view

Andy and his friends before the man at the oche, cigarette in mouth, squinted at the dartboard and expertly threw his dart into the treble twenty. After this brief inquisitorial interlude, the hubbub of conversation emanating from the ten or so customers resumed as quickly as it had been silenced.

Rupert, with the confidence born of several pints of beer, nudged his way up to the bar. 'Right chaps, my round. Lucinda, what's your tipple?'

'I'd better stick to gin and tonic please, Rupert, or I might end up legless.'

'You, Lucy?'

'Same, please.'

Rupert turned to the barman, 'And three pints of bitter, please.' Rupert leaned against the bar as the drinks were served, then picked up two of the pints and handed them to Nigel who was standing a little way off. 'Here, Nigel, take these, would you?'

As Nigel took the glasses, the barman caught his eye. 'Nige!' he exclaimed with surprise. 'Long time no see. So they let you out then?'

Nigel smiled weakly and just nodded. Lucy, who had been standing next to Nigel, turned to him and asked, 'You been here before?'

As he walked to a vacant table, he muttered, 'Maybe, a long time ago. Can't quite remember.'

'Wot does 'e mean *let you out*?'

Nigel hesitated for a moment. 'Oh, not sure, Luce. Probably out of university.'

Settled back at their table, Rupert raised his glass in a toast. 'Cheers, Andy. I haven't had such a good time in years.'

'Cheers, Rupert, you're all right for a toff.' Andy looked at Lucinda, 'You too. Cheers.'

After taking an elegant sip of her drink, Lucinda replied, 'How kind of you to say so, Andrew. You know,' she continued, glancing at Rupert, 'that's probably one of the nicest things anyone has said to me in a long time.'

''Ere's to the toffs.' Lucy lifted her glass slightly unsteadily and after following suit, they all toasted *the toffs*.

'Now I should like to propose a toast.' Lucinda paused as she hiccoughed, then said, 'The Clarms.'

'The Clarms,' echoed around the table.

During all of this bonhomie, none of them had noticed the solitary man in the long leather coat slowly sipping an orange juice on the other side of the room. They had not observed his approach either and it was only when he was standing alongside Nigel, who had not said much all evening, that Andy thought he vaguely recognised him; his thick bottle-bottom glasses seemed particularly familiar.

'Hello, Nigel,' he said quietly, his Irish lilt thick and heavy like a loaded gun. The stranger patted Nigel on the shoulder. 'Time off for good behaviour, was it?' The man's face was expressionless and sinister.

Nigel, whose normally rubicund face had changed to a shade of pale green, smiled weakly and simply nodded.

'No doubt you'll be wanting to pay back what you owe?'

Nigel nodded again.

'I'll be in touch then.' The leather-clad man then crossed the bar and disappeared silently into the night.

'Nigel,' said Lucinda, 'you seem to be awfully well known for someone who's never been here before.' Lucinda sipped her drink and smiled at Lucy.

'Yes, Nigel.' Lucy looked at him enquiringly. 'And wot's all this about being *out*?'

Nigel attempted to smile but simply managed a vacuous and insincere grin. 'I was away for a while. At university, you know, that sort of thing.' He took a swig from his pint glass, then looked at his watch. 'Good Lord! Look at the time.' he said brightly, 'I've an early start tomorrow so I'd better be getting along.' So saying, Nigel Bernard-Fielding rose from the table, gave Lucy a peck on the cheek, said he would give her a bell in the next day or two and then left.

As the door closed behind him, Lucinda turned to Lucy. 'Lucy dear, you never cease to amaze me. You're absolutely brilliant. You set the little fraud up, didn't you?'

'Well, a bit. But I didn't expect him to be a long-lost local celebrity.'

It was now approaching closing time and the landlord crossed to their table to take away the empty glasses. It was Rupert who engaged him in conversation. After a few pleasantries, he said, 'Our friend Nigel, the one who left a short while ago. You obviously know him well. He tells us that he's been away at university?'

The landlord looked at Rupert and smiled. 'Is *that* what they call it now?' Rupert nodded. 'Yeah, Pentonville

College!' He then turned to the other remaining occupants of the bar and shouted, 'Now, time, ladies and gents, *please*.'

It was Andy who broke the stunned silence. 'Away at university? What twaddle. It appears our friend Nigel Bernard-Fielding may have a slightly unsavoury past.' Andy resisted the temptation to smile.

'Are you terribly disappointed, Lucy dear?' Lucinda's face registered genuine concern.

'Not really, Lucinda. To be honest, I couldn't understand what 'e saw in me in the first place.'

'I hate to say it, Lucy dear, but I suspect he has some ulterior motive. His eyes are far too close together to be wholly trustworthy.'

'I always knew 'e was a twat, didn't I, Andy?'

'So you kept saying, Lucy. So you kept saying – a misunderstood twat!'

'Lucy dear, there is no question in my mind that you are far too good for him. If I were you, I would give him the sack with immediate effect.'

***

'Kenny, something big is going on.'

'What do you mean, Mick?'

'You'll never guess who I saw today.'

'Okay, Mick, stop muckin' about, just tell me what you saw, will you?'

'Well, firstly, Vinnie was in the Nellie, and guess who was with him?'

'Mick, I'm not in the mood for playing bleedin' guessing games.'

'Well, I'll tell you then. *Only*, Nigel.'

'What! Nigel B-F?'

'The very same: Nige the Con.' Mick nodded knowingly.

'So he's out, is he?'

'That's for sure. I seen him with me own eyes, Kenny.'

'Well, well, well. Don't time go quickly when you're enjoying yourself? He got ten years and with good behaviour, he'd be about due for parole. He owes you, doesn't he?'

'Ten grand he conned out of me and I intend to get it back. That's why I have stake in his next operation and that's the interesting thing, Kenny; Nigel and Vinnie are clearly hatching a plan as they were with two newcomers: a couple of tarts and a posh guy. I didn't recognise them but they'll be up to no good, that's for sure.'

'Some type of con, I should think. The tarts and the posh geezer will front the operation while Nigel gets to do the dirty on some poor bastard.'

'What about tomorrow, Kenny, do we still go ahead?'

'Yes, Mick. Vinnie needs to be put out of action. I can't have the borough thinking that people can shop me and get away with it.' Kenny was pensive for a moment. 'I thought you said that he was meeting in the Nelson?'

'They must have meant the Nellie. That's where he was tonight, for sure.'

'Good. We'll pay Mr Vinnie Bowman and his friend Nigel a visit tomorrow evening and this time, Mick, bring your shooter along.'

Chapter 18

History is made, not created. Coincidence and serendipity are the vital sparks in that primordial swamp that we call life. Statistical quirks, rather than conscious design, cause the events that eventually become our past. If Adam had not wandered out into the Garden of Eden just as Eve was taking a stroll or if it had been raining on that fateful day, then who knows what might have, or indeed might not have, happened. If Mr Marks had not met Mr Spencer, the world would be a different place. If Lennon had not palled up with McCartney, karaoke would be the poorer for it; but such is life, coincidence is what makes us, and allows us to evolve. It mixes our genes and makes life interesting. Put another way, if everything in life was totally predictable, our existence would be pretty mundane and boring.

Just as the crispness of the batter surrounding Andy's piece of plaice some three weeks earlier had fired off the totally unpredictable sequence of events that I am now relating, it was a series of unrelated occurrences that adversely influenced Andy's decision-making on the day of operation *Catch Kenny*, resulting in an outcome that could never have been predicted. It is said that real life is stranger than fiction. Certainly, no respectable writer of that particular genre would risk his credibility by penning a tale as unlikely as the one which unfolded that Thursday evening.

Firstly, Andy woke up with a hangover. After leaving the Nell Gwyn the previous night, the newly formed group of friends were in high spirits and felt that it would be a shame to curtail the evening. They, therefore, returned to Parkview and finished off a bottle of whisky that Andy had been saving for the New Year. Then Lucy found half a bottle of crème de menthe in her wardrobe, which she had been given for Christmas. When that had been consumed, they finished off the remains of a bottle of cooking sherry that Andy discovered under the sink.

Finally, at about three in the morning, Lucinda and Rupert phoned for a taxi, leaving Andy sound asleep on the couch. Lucy managed to negotiate the stairs, only to pass out on the landing. So it was that Andy set off for work the next day after just five hours of sleep, still inebriated and with a progressively worsening hangover. It was only at lunchtime that he remembered that this was the day of operation *Catch Kenny*. On a positive note, Andy's residual high blood alcohol level meant that his apprehension about the event was dulled; however, the downside of this state of affairs, as he later discovered, was that his cerebration was more than slightly under par.

At five o'clock, feeling only marginally better, Andy left work and, although tempted, walked past the Herald Lounge Bar and headed straight to Bank Station. He knew that he was supposed to be in position as a decoy at six o'clock and so, after exiting from Clapham Common tube station, he headed directly for the Nell Gwyn.

Yes, dear reader, you are well ahead of me. The Nell Gwyn was not the designated rendezvous as specified by the Chief Superintendent and his underling PC Crocker, which (you will recall) was the Lord Nelson. It was there that the full might of the Clapham police force was waiting, cunningly disguised, to protect Andy and hopefully effect the arrest of Kenny the Giant Craft. And what could be the reason for this fundamental error? Well, this is Andy Norris we are talking about, a man wandering aimlessly from one life-changing event to another without ever raising his eyes from the pavement, an individual meandering along the existential pathway without taking so much as a glimpse at the map of life.

A few days earlier, Andy had been told by Crocker that the trap, his role in which was to be the bait, was to be set in the Lord Nelson, a pub Andy rarely frequented. However, even before the interview was finished, this had been translated into 'The Nellie' in his own mind, a name by which that pub was often known. What was lost in translation was that in Andy's mind, the Nellie would always mean the Nell Gwyn so, within an hour or so of Crocker leaving Parkview, Andy had it firmly imprinted on his cortex that the sting operation was to be held in the Nell Gwyn. They say that communication, or the lack of it to be more specific, is the root cause of all evil. To put two pubs in the same vicinity, both of whose names could reasonably be shortened to "The Nellie", was stupidity in the most epic of proportions – but it happened: another example of the power of coincidence. If Alexander Fleming had not left his window open when he went away for, what was no doubt a well-deserved holiday, that penicillium spore would not have floated in from Praed Street to land on his exposed petri dish, an event that directly resulted in him receiving an all-expenses-paid trip to Stockholm some years later. But I digress: the final nail in this particular coffin of misunderstanding was that Andy had been in the Nell Gwyn the previous night with Lucy and her friends and in his suboptimal state of mentation, it never occurred to him to even consider that the trap might have been set in any other pub. So, without further consideration or conscious thought of any kind, Andy headed directly to Rookery Road and threw open the doors to the bar that he had left only eighteen hours before.

For a truly spectacular misunderstanding, two or more unrelated events need to be thrown together. Like two heavy sub-atomic particles colliding at high velocity, such occurrences result in secondary and tertiary incidents so totally unpredictable that they continue to affect circumstances until the end of time. Such is the nature of determinism. The second event in this particular sequence was the flawed presumption made by Myopic Mick that, because he had spotted the man who he thought was Vinnie Bowman in the Nell Gwyn the previous night, the meeting he had been told was scheduled for the Lord Nelson would also be in the Nell Gwyn. Now it is said that two rights do not make a wrong – or is it two wrongs do make a right? I am not quite sure, but there can be no doubt that the final twist of fate would have been if the police had also made the same mistake so that all parties involved in this little operation actually ended up in the wrong place but at the right time, resulting in the errors cancelling each other out (now that would have been truly serendipitous), but they did not. As instructed, the undercover policemen congregated in the Lord Nelson, a pub about half a mile further down Clapham Common Northside.

Thus it was that Andy, still somewhat bemused by the consumption of ten pints and several whiskies, a glass or two of crème de menthe along with a small sherry the night before, found himself in the Nell Gwyn with, amongst others, Myopic Mick and Kenny Craft; while a crack team of cunningly disguised police officers were in a pub less than a mile away, playing darts, joshing around and generally pretending to be having a good old time.

As Andy entered the Nell Gwyn, he was comforted to notice several other customers who, to the casual uninformed observer, looked like your average London drinkers having a pleasant time on their way home from work. There were a couple of old men playing darts and a few were sitting at tables while another group was standing chatting at the bar. Andy strolled in casually towards them, trying not to look at the other occupants. *Good disguises,* he thought to himself. *I'd never have guessed that these were highly trained, lethal, armed police officers.* Some, he noticed, even looked well past retirement age. He looked around to see if he could recognise Crocker and caught the eye of one or two of the customers, none of whom gave him more than a moment's attention. *Professional,* he thought, *very professional.* Seated in the corner of the room, he noticed the leather-coated man who had been there the previous evening. He was wearing a fedora and was squinting through thick glasses at a thin middle-aged man sitting beside him. *Thought as much: CID, as I predicted. Must have been involved with banging up Nigel,* he said to himself.

Confident in the knowledge that he was surrounded by a crack team of undercover policemen, Andy strolled nonchalantly to the bar and ordered a pint. The barman was the same one who had served him the previous night and, as he pulled his pint, Andy once again looked around at his fellow customers. *They really do look like a normal bunch of boozers,* he thought. 'Brilliant. You've got to hand it to the boys in blue: they are very good.' He smiled and winked discreetly at one in a knowing way, giving the impression that he understood who they were and that he too was playing his part in this conspiracy. In response, he received a blank stare. *Professional to the last,* he thought. *Well, if I'm going to be a decoy, I might as well make it good.* So he took his pint, sat at a table in a dark corner of the bar and, with an audible sigh, opened his *Evening News* and pretended to read.

Meanwhile, less than a mile away, the assembled group of plainclothes policemen were wondering where the star of the show was. Crocker, who was feeling a little chilly in his short trousers, put down his half pint of beer and glanced at his watch. Ten past seven. Crocker was worried. Andy Norris was now over an hour late. Maybe

Kenny had already got to the decoy. Maybe he had not waited to catch him in the pub but had dealt with him outside on the street or on the tube. A quick shove on to the line as a train arrives is all that it takes. He shivered. One or two of his colleagues seemed to be taking the joshing and having a good ol' time instruction a bit too literally and he suspected that several were already slightly inebriated. The two who looked like extras from a western, in particular, were swaying unsteadily near the bar.

Crocker looked around at his fellow officers and noticed one face that he did not recognise. He considered the situation for a moment. The fact that Mr Norris had not arrived did not necessarily mean that Kenny was not in the bar waiting for him. The only occupants of the bar were supposed to be his colleagues and here was an unidentified drinker sitting quietly at a table, a glass of whisky in front of him. He surreptitiously looked at the stranger, trying not to stare. *Could that be Kenny*, he wondered. The man was slightly built, looked to be dark-skinned, maybe of Indian origin, had a straggly beard and thinning grey hair. He appeared to be in his seventies, thus much older than the man he had questioned about a stolen bicycle all those months ago. In fact, he looked nothing at all like Kenny the Giant Craft, but it is an old adage that we all tend to believe what we want to believe and see what we want to see. Crocker desperately wanted this man to be Kenny Craft so, despite the absence of any significant similarity, he decided that the elderly Indian drinking whisky at the table must be the escaped prisoner in disguise. This momentous decision was based solely on the fact that he was the only man in the bar whom Crocker did not recognise. Suddenly, the fact that the stranger bore no resemblance whatsoever to his target did not matter. For Crocker, the man *had* to be Kenny purely because no one else was. Such was his flawed logic.

In fact, the unidentified man was an itinerant labourer who had been in the bar since lunchtime and was now steaming drunk. The first he knew of operation *Catch Kenny* was when he registered an oversized Boy Scout heading in his direction. He smiled vacantly at the approaching man, thinking it must be bob-a-job week, and was completely taken aback when the Scout yelled, 'Armed police', dropped down on one knee and pointed a revolver at his head. Behind the Boy Scout, to his amazement, there suddenly appeared a selection of bizarrely dressed men, many of whom were pointing guns in his direction.

In the space of a moment, the elderly labourer found himself pushed to the floor, handcuffed and frisked by two cowboys and what appeared to be an American tourist. 'There's nothing on him,' said one of the cowboys to Crocker. 'Are you sure this is the right man? Doesn't look much like the picture.'

Crocker rose from his shooting position, stepped forward and stared at the bemused man. He then bent down and tugged at the labourer's beard, which to his chagrin remained firmly attached to his face. Having failed to demonstrate that the beard was false, he vigorously rubbed his cheek in an attempt to reveal the man's true skin colour, which stubbornly remained dark. Crocker then slowly rose to his feet and stood stock-still as the awful truth slowly dawned on him. This was the wrong man: this man was not Kenny Craft. The man lying handcuffed on the floor in front of him did not even look like Kenny Craft. Crocker was silent for a while as he looked at the expectant faces of his fellow officers. Then, as though nothing untoward had occurred, he calmly said, 'Sorry, chaps, wrong man. Back to your posts.'

As his colleagues put away their guns and drifted back to the bar, Crocker addressed the labourer who had sobered up remarkably quickly. 'PC Crocker, Clapham Police,' he said while showing the man his warrant card. 'Sorry about that, sir, but you have an uncanny resemblance to an escaped prisoner we were hoping to apprehend.' While unlocking the handcuffs, Crocker offered to buy the man a drink to compensate him for the inconvenience of nearly being shot, but the man, once released of his shackles, simply ran out of the door and did not stop until he reached the Common, where he found a vacant park bench sat down and vowed never, ever, to have another drink.

Back in the Nell Gwyn, Andy was beginning to suspect that all was not as it should be. He had a strange feeling similar to one he had last experienced when he had attended the wrong funeral by mistake. He recalled how, standing at the back of the church, gradually the realisation had dawned on him that he did not recognise a single face in the congregation and even the name of the deceased was unfamiliar to him. Such was the feeling that he was now experiencing as he sat in the Nell Gwyn waiting to be shot.

He glanced around the bar at the other customers; looking for a reassuring familiar face, even a glimpse of Crocker, would have been welcome. He then noticed that several of the customers had finished their drinks and left, leaving only a small group of four men standing chatting at the bar.

Andy was feeling even more uneasy. He decided to investigate and headed over to the group. As he stood at the bar waiting to be served, without turning his head, he muttered out of the side of his mouth to the man standing next to him, 'How's it going then? Any sign of the Giant?'

The man, clearly surprised by this comment from a complete stranger, turned and said, 'I beg your pardon?'

Andy, still staring directly ahead, repeated his question but now a degree of urgency was noticeable in his tone. 'I said, any sign of the Giant?' He then turned and winked at the man in an obvious fashion.

'There're no giants here, mate.' The bemused drinker then turned his back on Andy and edged a little further along the bar. Andy was now becoming desperately concerned. This was not the response he had expected from a highly trained, armed police officer, and when the little group of drinkers emptied their glasses and left the pub, the awful truth began to dawn on him. Something had gone badly awry and he was now alone in the bar except for the two strange-looking men in the corner. His blood ran cold and he froze.

'Same again, mate?'

The barman's voice slowly penetrated Andy's consciousness and he realised that the barman was staring at him.

Without thinking, Andy said,' Yes, please,' and handed over his pint mug.

From their position seated at a table in the corner of the bar, Mick and Kenny had been watching, biding their time. 'Now's our chance, Kenny.' Myopic Mick looked at his friend. 'Whenever you want, Kenny. Just say the word.' He patted the bulge in his coat pocket in a sinister fashion.

Kenny glanced at the man at the bar. Certainly, he was untidy, overweight and bore a resemblance to Vinnie Archer but the light was poor and he was concerned that something did not quite add up. 'Right, let's go, but I want to see him close up before you pull the trigger. Got that, Mick?'

'For sure. Just say the word.' The two of them rose and headed towards Andy who was standing stock-still, rigid with fear, at the bar. The next thing Andy Norris knew was that someone had put an arm around his shoulder and was talking to him in a quietly menacing voice. 'Good evening, Vinnie, 'ave you missed me?' Andy turned to face the speaker and two things happened simultaneously. Firstly, he saw the leather-clad, bespectacled man in the fedora pointing the barrel of a gun at his bulging midriff while at the same time, the man with his arm around his shoulder was staring at him, an expression of surprise and complete disbelief on his face. 'Who the hell are you?' exclaimed the man.

Initially lost for words, Andy eventually managed to spit out, 'A-Andy Norris.'

Kenny removed his arm and stood back. 'Mick, you bloody idiot, this is the wrong man. For Christ's sake, put that gun away.'

'What d'you mean, the wrong man?'

'I mean the *wrong man*. That is, he is a member of that vast army of men who are *not* Vinnie Archer. Put the bloody gun away.' Kenny looked along the bar to where the barman was pulling Andy's pint, oblivious to what was going on just a few yards away.

Mick put the gun back in his pocket and squinted closely at Andy. 'Are you sure? It looks like him, Kenny.'

'Mick, you imbecile, you've been trying to kill the wrong man.'

'He looks like Vinnie – you've got to admit that, Kenny. Particularly from a distance.'

The barman put Andy's pint on the bar. 'That'll be one ten, mate.'

Andy, who had not moved a muscle throughout the whole of these exchanges, could only mutter, 'Uh!'

Kenny reached for his wallet. 'My round,' he said as he handed a five-pound note to the barman before adding, 'Another two pints as well, please, mate.'

By now, Andy was not in a good state mentally: in fact, he had become catatonic. His emotions had been battered by a crazy roller-coaster ride where one moment he was in a room full of men whom he had thought were undercover policemen; the next, he was alone apart from a shortsighted assassin and an escaped prisoner. He no longer knew what to believe and what to disbelieve. Just seconds ago, a leather-clad Irishman and an angry Londoner were about to shoot him and now one of his erstwhile assassins was buying him a drink. He looked at the man called Kenny. 'Forgive me for asking, but are you going to shoot me?'

'No, mate. Whatever gave you that idea?'

'The gun – mainly.'

'That's just Mick getting a bit overenthusiastic.' After the barman had delivered the beers, Kenny whispered to Andy, 'I don't know who you are, mate, but it would be helpful if you kept quiet about this little business with the gun an' all.'

'Uh?'

'It's just that you're not the man Mick here thought you were.'

Andy managed to find his voice. 'Sorry about that.'

'That's all right. It's not your fault, mate.' Kenny swallowed a mouthful of beer. 'I suspect Mick has caused you some inconvenience for which he apologises. Don't you, Mick?'

'For sure. I'm sorry, whoever you are. My eyesight's not what it used to be. You do look a lot like Vinnie though, from a distance at least. You're right though, Kenny. I could probably do with getting some new spectacles.'

'Let me get this straight,' Andy said to Kenny. 'You trusted this man,' and he glanced at Mick. 'This man – a man with bilateral Jodrell Banks for glasses – to identify me and then shoot me because he thought I was someone else?'

'That's just about it, yeah. It's a good job I was here; otherwise, you'd be dead by now, even though you don't look anything like Vinnie close up.'

Mick prodded Andy in the chest. 'Okay, I accept that you're not Vinnie the Bowman close up, but what were you doing in here last night consorting with Nigel the con and the rest of your gang? Explain that to me, Mr *I'm not Vinnie Archer* Norris. Eh!'

'Uh?' Andy had reverted to monosyllables.

'The people you were with last night.'

'They were friends of Lucy's.'

'What's Lucy's game then? Soliciting?'

'Well, in a way, I suppose. She's a legal secretary.'

Kenny then interrupted. 'Mick, shut up. You've caused enough trouble for one night. This man is *not* Vinnie and that's all that matters.' Kenny turned to Andy, 'Another beer, mate? It's Mick's round, isn't it, Mick?' Kenny turned to the barman. 'Three more pints, please.'

The barman looked at Kenny as he pulled the first pint. 'Did I hear that you're looking for Vinnie Archer?'

Kenny looked at the barman with interest. 'Yes, he's an old friend. D'you happen to know where I might find him?'

'In a freezer, mate. He died three weeks ago. 'Ad an 'eart attack.'

Slowly Kenny's face creased into a wide smile. 'Well, well! Vinnie's dead. I should have guessed.'

Andy still could not understand how operation *Catch Kenny* had gone so badly wrong but he was now beginning to relax. He had narrowly avoided getting shot and that threat now seemed to have receded once and for all. 'My round, I think,' he said, 'Kenny, Mick, same again?'

'Shouldn't we be going, Kenny?' Mick asked nervously.

'No, Mick. I'm enjoying myself. This is the first night out I've had for three weeks, and we should toast Vinnie's health – or rather the lack of it.'

Chapter 19

After the unfortunate Indian labourer had left and the undercover squad had returned to their posts, both on the oche and at the bar, Crocker began to suspect that something had gone awry with operation *Catch Kenny*. As he wracked his brains for the smallest of flaws in this well-organised and watertight plan, he vaguely recalled Andy calling this pub The Nellie.

The landlord of the Lord Nelson had been taken aback when the strange assortment of police officers had arrived at six o'clock and was slightly concerned that one of his lunchtime customers had nearly been shot so when the oversized Scout approached him, he was in no frame of mind to moderate his opinion of the operation thus far. 'Look, mate, you and your men are giving this pub a bad name. I've got my reputation to think of.'

Crocker leant his staff against the bar. 'Sorry about that: just a case of mistaken identity. Happens all the while in my line of work. Now tell me, landlord, is there another pub called the Lord Nelson around here?'

'No, mate. This is the only one in the vicinity.'

'How about another pub called the Nellie?'

'Sure. There's the Nell Gwyn just down the road.'

On hearing this, Crocker just stared at the landlord from below the rim of his Scout hat. Slowly at first, then ever more quickly, the significance of what he had just heard gradually penetrated Crocker's slightly addled brain. After a few moments, he asked the landlord once more, his voice slow and deliberate with *gravitas.* 'Are you saying that there's another pub called the Nellie just down the road?'

'Yes, mate, that's exactly what I'm saying. Now d'you want a drink or not?'

Crocker, his face pale, turned to face his colleagues. 'Lads,' he shouted. Then, as silence descended, he addressed them quietly and slowly. 'Men, I think we're in the wrong pub.'

A gasp of disbelief could be heard from those assembled in the room. 'There's another pub down the road called the Nell Gwyn. I think Mr Norris is there at this very moment, in imminent danger of his life. We need to get there as quickly as possible.' Crocker then picked up his staff and rushed to the door of the pub, followed by his motley crew.

As the door slammed shut behind them, the landlord heaved a sigh of relief. 'Thank God for that,' he announced to the now empty room as he began to collect the empty glasses.

Crocker and his men ran most of the way to the Nell Gwyn and arrived about fifteen minutes later, panting after their unexpected exertion. Gathered outside, they discussed their options in hushed whispers. 'I think we should storm the place,' said one of the cowboys.

'Too dangerous,' said another, 'there might be a hostage situation in there.'

One of the pretend businessmen then suggested, 'We could lay siege to the pub. You know, till they run out of food.'

'Don't be an idiot,' retorted one of the men in short sleeves who was already feeling the cold. 'That could take weeks.'

'We need to know what's going on inside,' said Crocker, who was jumping up and down trying to peer through a window above the doorway. 'Here! Lift me up,' he said and he was hoisted on to the back of one of his colleagues. Just then, a dapper elderly man out for his evening constitutional and a small libation, calmly said, 'Excuse me,' as he squeezed past the two policemen, then opened the door and entered the pub.

On noticing this, Crocker had a flash of genius. That instant in time, the eureka moment, that separates the likes of him to the rest of us mere mortals. 'That's it!' exclaimed Crocker as the door swung closed behind the old man and he dismounted from the back of his fellow officer. 'My disguise is impenetrable. I'll just walk in nonchalantly and check whether Norris and Kenny are in there.'

So saying, Crocker adjusted his hat, took his forked staff firmly in his hand and with a curt, 'Wait here for me; I'll whistle when I know it's safe to come in,' to his companions, headed boldly through the door of the Nell Gwyn. Once inside, he glanced around. At the bar was the elderly man being served, while across the room, he identified three men sitting at a table laughing and joking. One of them looked familiar and it was with massive relief that Crocker realised it was Andy Norris who appeared not only to be alive, but to be in the best of health. Without hesitation, Crocker walked directly up to the table where the three of them were sitting and sat down next to Andy Norris.

'Mr Norris,' he said, 'thank God you're all right. We've been waiting for you in another pub down the road.' He then looked up at Andy's two companions. 'Are these your friends?'

Andy, as you will remember, was still not at his intellectual best. He had started the day with a crashing hangover and since six o'clock, had had a gun pointed at him, had narrowly escaped being shot and by now had drunk five pints of the local ale. With such a tenuous grasp on reality, the last thing that he needed was a total stranger, who appeared to be a scoutmaster, wearing short trousers and carrying a staff, sit down next to him and tell him that he had been waiting for him in another pub. It is just this sort of occurrence that can drive a man over the edge.

Andy, his eyes now red-rimmed and glazed by the events of the last 48 hours, looked at the man wearing the Baden-Powell hat. There was something familiar about his appearance but he could not make out what. Kenny and Mick, meanwhile, simply stared disbelievingly at the man for several moments before Kenny turned to Andy Norris and said, 'Andy, you should have said you were due at a Scout meeting.'

'I wasn't.'

'This man says you were. Are you in the Scouts or not?'

Andy put his head in his hands and sighed. 'To be honest, Kenny, after what's been going on today, for all I know, I might be a member of the Ku-Klux-Klan.'

'I didn't know the Ku-Klux-Klan had a branch in Clapham,' said Mick, draining his glass before turning to his partner and adding, 'Kenny, I really do think it's time we should go.'

Two things now happened simultaneously. Crocker, on hearing the leather-clad man address his friend as Kenny, suddenly realised that his quarry was sitting within an arm's length of him on the opposite side of the table; while at exactly the same moment, Andy realised who the Scout was. If Andy had been thinking more quickly, he would not have chosen that moment to shout out, '*Good God*! It's you, Crocker.' but mentally he was not at his best – and he did.

As Crocker recognised Kenny and Andy recognised Crocker, a strange thing happened. Kenny looked up from his glass at Crocker and said resignedly, 'Crocker, I've got to hand it to you. You're good; you're *very* good.' He then rested his hands on the table in a gesture of surrender. 'Somehow I don't mind getting nabbed by a cop like you.' He turned and looked at his hitman. 'It's all over, Mick. I told you 'e was good, didn't I?'

'For sure. That's a cunning outfit. There's no shame in being caught by such a master of disguise. It's a privilege to be arrested by you, Mr Crocker.' Mick then removed the gun from his pocket and placed it on the table in front of

Crocker. 'It's a pity I didn't get a chance to put the frighteners on Nigel though.' The pair of them then offered Crocker their wrists.

Crocker was slightly taken aback. Swinging from his belt were several items essential for any Scout, including a penknife (which had that really useful attachment for getting stones out of horses' hooves), a whistle, a torch and a tool for digging latrines. However, useful as these items undoubtedly were, at that precise moment, he would have happily swapped them all for a pair of handcuffs, which were not standard Scouting issue. Then, in a moment of inspiration, he untied the lanyard from around his neck and drew it tight around the two men's wrists. He then picked up Mick's gun and blew loudly on his whistle to indicate that his colleagues should enter.

As fifteen strangely dressed policemen, some carrying pistols, entered the bar, Kenny was heard to mutter, 'Clever! Very clever.'

***

'Lucy dear, you'll never guess what!'

It was Friday evening and Lucy, alone in Parkview, had answered the phone. 'Lucinda, you sound very excited.'

'I am. Rupert's proposed to me at last. And it's all down to you and your friend, Andrew.'

'That's great, but 'ow's it got anythin' to do with us?'

'It was on Wednesday or (more accurately) the early hours of Thursday morning after our night out with you in

Clarm. He proposed to me in the taxi on the way back to my place.'

'And you said yes?'

'Of course I did.' Lucinda fell silent for a moment. 'The only slight problem was that he couldn't remember asking me the next morning and needed a little reminder of the events of the previous night.'

'And?'

'Well, he didn't deny it. To be absolutely honest, he did need a little prompting in the first place. But I know he wanted to propose; it's just that he's a trifle shy.'

'Wot d'you mean, a little *prompting*?'

'Well,' Lucinda hesitated, 'He needed some encouragement so I told him to propose to me.'

'Let me get this straight. You *told* him to propose?'

'Yes.'

'And he did?'

'Well, in a fashion.'

'Wot sort of fashion?'

'Well, he was having problems with his speech by that time, as you may remember, so I said, "Do you want me to marry you?" and he didn't answer. So I told him to nod if he meant yes and he did. Although it's just possible that might have had something to do with the fact that the taxi went over a bump in the road at that very moment. But it matters not. The fact remains that he proposed and I accepted. Next morning, after I'd reminded him a few times, he became quite resigned to the idea. Anyway, he'd be wasted on anyone else.'

'Well, Lucinda. I don't know wot to say.'

'Sometimes, Lucy darling, men just have to be told what they need to do because they're not very good at thinking for themselves.'

'You are so right, Lucinda. Congratulations. Big wedding?'

'No, just a few hundred, then back to our place for a bit of a bash. You'll be invited, of course.'

'Where will it be?'

'You've probably heard of it, a place called Westminster Abbey. It's an old family tradition.'

'Cor!'

'Anyway, darling, enough about me. How's your undercover agent? The whole of that evening is ever so slightly vague, but I seem to recall that he was involved in some hush-hush police operation the night after our little pub crawl.'

'Yeah, it's a long story but Andy's a bit of a local hero actually. It appears that he kept two dangerous villains talking for several hours until the police came and arrested them. There was a bit of a shootout but luckily no one was hurt.'

'Gosh, how exciting! It all goes on in Clarm, doesn't it? I think Rupert and I have had all the excitement we can cope with for the time being.'

'It's all in the papers: pictures and everything. The arresting officer was dressed as a Boy Scout.'

'Lucy dear, how exciting. How is Andrew coping with this newfound fame?'

'Very well, actually. That's mainly 'cos he can't remember much about it but that's normal for him.'

'Oh, do give him my congratulations. I think he's an absolute dear. Not as good a catch as my Rupert of course, but an absolute dear, nonetheless.'

'D'you think so?'

'Of course, Lucy dear, he's so charmingly unaffected. I love that. Anyway, what about that awful fraud, Nigel? Tell all.'

'I think you were right, Lucinda. He hasn't been seen at work since Wednesday.'

'I hate to say I told you so, Lucy, but, as you know, I suspected he was a fraud. Consider it a lucky escape. Rodney says that he was trying to access the legal records of several clients: highly sensitive issues like divorce, tax evasion, wills, that sort of thing, probably to use for the purpose of blackmail or conning innocent folk out of their money. Lucy, you'll hate me for saying this but I suspect, in you, he saw someone who might be able to assist him in his misdeeds.'

'Now you come to mention it, Lucinda, I think you're right. He did ask me to get him some files for which he had no legitimate need but luckily, all of them were designated "partner access only", so I couldn't help him.'

'There you are, just as I suspected. I can always tell. His eyes were far too close together, a sure sign of a criminal nature. Now take Rupert's eyes, for example: they're miles apart. Sometimes I think he must have three-hundred-and-sixty-degree vision. Ugly, yes, but honest. A man with eyes that far apart couldn't possibly commit a crime: it's a physical impossibility. Worst of all, though, Nigel was a social climber. Those are the ones to watch, Lucy dear, unlike your Andrew who couldn't care less.'

'He's not *my* Andy.'

'Whatever. I must go now as I have wedding plans to make and Rupert needs constant reminding that he's engaged to me. He still seems a trifle unsure but I'm absolutely convinced it's what he wants. It's just that he doesn't necessarily know it yet.'

'Doesn't love come into it?'

'*Love*? Oh, Lucy dear, how quaint. No, absolutely not. Marriage is far too important an estate to allow mere transient human emotions to get involved. That's what lovers and mistresses are for. You can't allow love and sex to mess up a perfectly good marriage. And besides, we're talking about a Fourteenth Earl: the aristocracy in particular have to be told what to do. They haven't thought for themselves in generations, for heaven's sake. Well, I must go now. Take care.'

Chapter 20

'Hey, man, is you sure?'

'Read it for yourself, Zeph.' Andy passed over his copy of the *London Evening News* where the headlines read, *Escaped criminal caught in daring pub raid.*

Zephaniah read the story while moving his lips to the words. 'Hey, is that you, Andy? It says here that a brave south London boozer detained a well-known armed gangster until the police arrived.'

'I am that man.' Andy nodded modestly.

'It says you is a hero.'

'So I believe.'

'Wait till I tell Mrs Zephaniah that I know a real-life hero.'

'Are you going to tell both of them?'

'One at a time, man, I don't want them getting overexcited.' Zephaniah put his copy of the *Racing Times* down on the table. 'Anyway, man, how did you detain them?'

'To be honest, Zeph, once they realised that I wasn't the man they wanted to kill, they were really good company. Mick, that's the Irish assassin, bought me a beer and we had a long chat about the Irish problem, job opportunities, the miners' strike, deteriorating visual acuity – things like that. I even suggested having a game of darts but Kenny, that's the escaped prisoner, vetoed the idea as being too dangerous with Mick being so shortsighted. Then a Boy Scout walked in and calmly arrested the two of them.'

'Is they allowed to do that?'

'Who?'

'Boy Scouts. Is it a new badge? *Competent Criminal Catching.*'

'No Zeph, he wasn't a real Boy Scout; it was PC Crocker in disguise. A master of disguise, that man.'

'So is it safe to be seen with you now, man, or is you still a walking death trap?'

'Absolutely safe, Zeph. It's business as usual. Back to the *status quo.*'

'Okay then, man, it's your round. Rum and coke for me, please.'

Andy wandered to the bar. 'Don't suppose you want to hear Mrs Mills playing Christmas tunes? It's still on the jukebox.'

'If you put that on, I is personally goin' to kill you, one hundred per cent. Now get me that drink.'

***

'Crocker, I have to admit that I've had my doubts about you in the past but you have certainly excelled yourself on this occasion.' The Chief Superintendent sat back in his swivel chair and placed the tips of his fingers together.

'Not only did we nab Kenny, but we also got that Irish hitman as a bonus. Eh!'

'Thank you, sir.' Crocker was standing in front of the chief's desk, looking modestly at the floor. 'There was a certain amount of good fortune involved, sir.'

'Nonsense, Crocker. My plan worked like clockwork.'

'Apart from the fact that we were in the wrong pub, sir.'

'No, Crocker; you were *not* in the wrong pub. The decoy and the target were in the wrong pub. We cannot take responsibility for the ineptitude of others, now, can we?'

'No, sir.'

'Besides, that's a mere detail. The plan was executed perfectly. And I must say you did well, Crocker. Very well. And d'you know why, Crocker?'

PC Crocker was about to respond when the Chief Super continued, 'I'll tell you why. It's because you're regular, that's why. I've never known someone who's not regular make a good police officer.'

'Absolutely, sir.'

'Now that Kenny's back inside, I should be up for promotion, I should think.' The Chief swivelled in his chair to add emphasis to his point.

Crocker coughed. 'And me, sir?'

The problem with you, Crocker, is that there is still the outstanding business of the stolen bicycle.'

'The one with a silver frame, drop handlebars and pink mudguards?'

'The very one. Solve that and there'll be some sergeant's stripes to sew on, Crocker.'

'I'll get on to it right away, sir.' And PC Crocker turned and left the Chief Superintendent's office.

***

It was a fine evening so Andy decided to eat his plaice and chips on the park bench near Clapham Common tube station. Sitting at the other end of the bench was someone he had not seen before: an elderly Indian gentleman with a grey beard and thinning white hair wearing workman's clothing. Andy offered his opened package of fish and chips. 'Chip, mate?'

The man seemed a trifle surprised but leant forward, thanked him and helped himself to a chip. Andy peered at him intently. He looked like an elderly itinerant labourer but after the events of the last few days, Andy realised that all was not necessarily as it first seemed. He peered closely at his companion on the bench; then after a moment's uncertainty, asked, 'Is that you, Crocker?'

On hearing this, the man's eyes widened. He held up his hands and shouted, 'Don't shoot,' then sprang to his feet and raced off down the road. Bemused, Andy once more reached into yesterday's *Evening News* and saw, underneath what remained of his large portion of plaice and chips, the picture of a man that bore an uncanny resemblance to himself. Puzzled, he looked more closely. No, it was not him, but an older version. He cleared some fish away to reveal the legend beneath the picture, which read, *London Gangster Vinnie the Bowman Archer Dies of heart attack*. Andy smiled to himself, finished the last piece of plaice and decided that when he got back to Parkview, he would ask Lucy if she wanted to come to the darts match with him the following night.